THE SCANDALOUS WIDOW

Monette Cummings

Masquerading as a widow whose husband had been killed at war, lovely young Ariel set off for London with her cousin, Clare, determined to take Society by storm. And so she did – but not in the way she had anticipated! Trapped in her disguise, the vivacious "widow" found herself forced into yet another role, one which seemed certain to tarnish her reputation and ruin her chances of winning the love of Lord Dexter, to whom she had secretly given her heart!

THE SCANDALOUS WIDOW

Monette Cummings

Curley Publishing, Inc.
South Yarmouth, Ma.

CUM
LARGE
PRINT

Library of Congress Cataloging-in-Publication Data available

Published in Large Print by arrangement with Dorchester Publishing, Inc. in the United States, Canada, the U.K. and British Commonwealth.

Distributed in Great Britain, Ireland and the Commonwealth by CHIVERS LIBRARY SERVICES LIMITED, Bath BA1 3HB, England.

Printed in Great Britain

ONE

"That is precisely what I mean, Clare," the older girl said for perhaps the dozenth time. "A widow is allowed to have so much more freedom than an unmarried girl."

"But you are not a widow, so that cannot signify," Clarissa protested as she had done before.

Ariel sighed and shook her head. She had known from the beginning that it was going to be a difficult task to bring her cousin to her point of view, but she had almost reached the place where she thought that it would be impossible to accomplish such a thing.

Clare had the sweetest disposition of anyone Ariel had ever known and she was not a stupid person; far from it. She had always been quick to grasp the few lessons which Ariel had been permitted to teach her and she could run a household better than many women twice her age.

The trouble with her – or at least it had always appeared troublesome in the opinion of her cousin – was that Clarissa not only looked like the pictures she had seen of angels, with her golden ringlets and her cornflower blue

1

eyes, she would also, if left to her own devices, behave like one. There was not an ounce of guile in her entire being.

It was Ariel who had the stronger spirit of the two and it had always been she who had led the younger girl into mischief. Still, she had always been honest enough to shoulder the blame if they were caught out. This happened all too frequently for it was Ariel's habit to plunge headlong into whatever scheme entered her head, without giving the slightest thought to the consequences.

Now she went through her latest plan once more, explaining each step with care.

"You are right, of course, Clare – I am not a widow. But I shall *pretend* that I am one. Let me see; do you think that I ought to say that I am the widow of a very rich, very old man who left all his property to me when he died? No – I think it would be better if I pretended that I was the widow of a soldier. There must be so many of them that one could not question it. Has it been long enough since Waterloo, do you think, that no one would think it strange that I have put off my mourning? Perhaps not; let us say that he fell at Talavera instead. Is that not a wondrous plan?"

"You cannot be serious," Clarissa said, but a familiar sinking sensation deep within her said that Ariel was all too serious about this mad scheme of hers – and that *she* would somehow be drawn into it, no matter what she might say.

Ariel could say that she was only pretending, but actually, she would be living a lie. This was the way her scheme looked to Clarissa – and she would be doing the same if she could not dissuade her cousin from going through with it.

She had seen from the beginning that Ariel had that mischievous look in her eyes. Clarissa knew it only too well, having seen it every time that Ariel got some wild idea into her brain.

It had been Ariel who had led her out to climb trees when they ought to have been baking bread. Both of them had torn their gowns and not only had they been whipped soundly for the prank, they had gone to bed supperless because there was no bread and had been forced to wear their much mended gowns for months before Uncle Sylvester would allow them to have new ones.

It was Ariel who had taken a dare from one of the village lads to go rafting on the duck pond and had dragged Clarissa with her – with the result that both of them had tumbled into the water, which fortunately had not been deep, and had been returned to Sylvester's wrathful care covered with mud and slime. Ariel never cared what punishment she received for her pranks – only being sorry that Clarissa must be punished as well – as long as she could have the fun of them beforehand.

Now, of course, there was no longer anyone to catch them out and punish them if they did wrong, no one to keep Ariel from doing exactly what she pleased.

"Why should I not do it?" Ariel was demanding now, laughing. "Only think of it, Clare – all of these years, we have lived less than two days' journey from London and have never had a chance to see it, or to go anywhere else, for that matter. When have we ever been given the chance to do anything? And it has not been the lack of money which has kept us down, either. It was pure miserliness. And now, all the money is mine, to do with as I please."

Clarissa was aware that it would do no good to tell Ariel that her entire plan was wrong, for that would only encourage her to go on with it. She did say unhappily, "I cannot think that it is the right thing to speak of miserliness – now."

Ariel touched the tiny frown which had appeared on her cousin's forehead with a gentle finger, as if to smooth it away.

4

"Dearest Clare – you would say nothing but good of anyone, no matter what the reason. But the truth is that Uncle Sylvester *was* a miser, and the fact that he is gone now cannot change that fact. The only thing which surprises me, now that I know of my fortune, is that he did not think to tie the money up in some fashion so that I still could not take complete possession of it."

Even with the best will in the world, Clarissa could not bring herself to deny that her cousin was right. Sylvester Morwin would most certainly have tied up his niece's fortune if he could have found some way of doing so and if it had occurred to him that he would not be about for many more years to see that she did not squander it.

"I only hope," she whispered, "that he cannot know what she plans to do now." She was certain that he would not be able to rest if he did so.

It was not that Sylvester would have trusted his niece less than anyone else. In his mind, almost everyone had a tendency, which almost amounted to the criminal, to waste precious money.

Sylvester had managed to raise both his nieces, Ariel from less than a month after her fifth birthday, Clarissa from the age of eight, without having to expend as much as a penny

5

from his own far from inconsiderable fortune.

Ariel's father, although he could not have had an inkling of the carriage accident which was to take his life, had been a more farsighted man than his brother-in-law. Ariel was his sole heiress; a firm in London which had managed his finances would do the same for her until she came of age – and afterward, should she wish it – while her mother's brother would care for her.

He had some slight qualms about this last, for he had some knowledge of Sylvester's saving ways, but there was no other relative to whom he might entrust her. His lordship thought that he had managed to circumvent any objections Mr. Morwin might raise by arranging for a large income to be paid each month. This would handily cover any expenses which Ariel might incur, so that her upkeep would not be a burden upon her uncle.

What he could not have foreseen, however, was the fact that Mr. Morwin, when he was apprised of the amount of the monthly income, had decided that it could easily pay all his expenses as well as those of his niece. When his brother's daughter was orphaned, she was added to the menage with no expenditure from Sylvester's pocket.

Ariel's income was large enough to supply

the three of them with all necessities – and, in his opinion, it only spoilt young females to be given such fripperies as modish gowns and bonnets. The clothing which he permitted them to have was serviceable – which meant that it hung upon their growing forms when new, was almost uncomfortably tight by the time he decided that they might discard it, was warm enough for winter and unpleasantly hot in summer – and was invariably of those ugly colours which would show the least wear.

"You should be thankful for all that you have," he told them often. "Think of all the poor children who have so much less than you."

When Ariel had first come to him, he had been forced to employ a housekeeper, being unable to care for a small child by himself. However, by the time Clarissa arrived, Ariel was nearly eleven and the housekeeper was dismissed – only too thankful, she declared to all who would listen, to go somewhere where she would not be starved.

"You are now old enough to manage the house," Sylvester told his elder niece, "and the child can handle many of the simpler tasks for you. Children much younger than either of you are working in mines and factories. You should be thankful that you have such an easy life. And a few duties may serve to keep you out of mischief."

Neither the "few duties" – which meant the care of the house, the garden, sewing, cooking, and marketing – nor the frequent applications of Sylvester's riding crop when these were shirked could keep Ariel from getting into mischief.

She could only remember her father, a bluff, good-natured man who had been determined to make up to his daughter for the loss of the mother who had died at her birth. There were other pleasant memories – of a fat pony which had come as a birthday present, dolls with silken gowns, of servants who cosseted her and tried to anticipate her slightest wish.

The memories had faded with the years until she could no longer be certain if they were real or only dreams for, during the years that the housekeeper had remained, she had not the leisure for cosseting anyone and, deciding that dolls and ponies were unnecessary extravagances which would only teach the child to expect more of the same, Sylvester had sold them all, putting the money carefully away in case of need.

Clarissa had been old enough to remember both of her parents very well and often thought of how happy the three of them had been, although they had never had much money. What they had was spent freely, however, and what they had laughingly referred to as their poverty was luxury compared to the life she found under her uncle's roof.

"I feed the pair of you and keep a good roof over your heads," he often declared. "You cannot expect me to do anything more. I am not made of money."

When Ariel had first come to him, Sylvester – because he had once rashly promised her father to see that she received an education – had found a young woman who, for the few pennies he would give her, was willing to teach the girl to read and write. That was all the education any female required, in his opinion; anything more would only serve to make her discontented with her lot in life.

He had dispensed with the woman's services several years before Clarissa entered his household and was happy to learn that her education had proceeded to a point where it would not be necessary to spend money for a teacher for her. Ariel could supply any lack in her education. He generously consented to permit them to read the few books in his possession when such pastimes did not interfere with their duties, but he saw to it that they had little time for such indulgences.

9

The will left by the Earl of Watling had specified that Ariel was to come into full control of her fortune upon her eighteenth birthday or upon her marriage, should that come sooner. Sheltered as the girls had been, there was very little chance that she would be married, despite the fact that their nearest neighbor, with his eye upon Mr. Morwin's acres, had continued to call, defying all Sylvester's attempts to discourage him.

Thinking – and with good reason – that if a girl who had never had a penny of her own to spend was suddenly informed that she had an almost unlimited fortune at her command, she would certainly spend a great deal of it upon frivolous clothing and other unnecessary things, Sylvester had never told Ariel that she was an heiress. He had also been in correspondence with the London firm which managed her money, advising them merely to continue sending her usual income and nothing more.

"There is no need for her to have more than this to spend while she is beneath my roof," he had written. "And the additional money would only prove a burden to her at this time. Should she come to London" – and he was determined that this should not happen – "she will find use enough for it then."

It would have been a simple matter for

10

Sylvester to have asked for an increase in the allowance and to have pocketed the money, but he would not do so. With so much money at hand, even he might have been tempted to spend some of it. In all the years Ariel had lived in his house, he had never retained a penny of her money. Paying his own and Clarissa's expenses from her income he had felt was his right, in return for supplying the girl with a home. If a shilling or two happened to be left over at the time the next check arrived, it was scrupulously put away, in case it might be needed one day.

It was not until he had been carried off by a chill – having decided, despite the unusually cold weather, that it was too late in the season to have a fire anywhere in the house – that Ariel, in going through his papers, had found the letters from MacPherson and Son which informed her that, for the past six months, she had been mistress of a considerable fortune.

"Only think of it, Clare," she cried now. "Never again must we have ugly gowns, just because they wear well. And there was never any need for us to have done so. We could have afforded the best of everything. And now, that is just what we shall have: the most expensive, the most elegant gowns to

11

be found in London – and everything else we wish, as well."

"But we cannot wear such things now – it would not be right – not until we are out of mourning."

"Out of mourning? That should be at once. I consider that Uncle Sylvester has been keeping us in mourning all these years, and I, for one, had had more than enough of all these unpleasant things. I am ready for a spree."

"Spree?" Clarissa was shocked. "Ariel, where do you learn these dreadful cant expressions?"

Ariel broke into a laugh. "Now, how do you know that it is a cant term?" she teased.

"Well, I only thought that it must be, for it sounds so – so –"

Her embarrassment brought another laugh, for Ariel was pleased with everything today.

"As a matter of fact," she admitted, "I think that you may be right about it, for Henry used it one time and then looked so shocked at having allowed it to slip out that I teased him into telling me just what it means."

"Ariel, you did not –"

"Certainly I did, and it is nothing so bad, after all. It simply means an enjoyable time. Of course I should imagine that, with gentlemen, an enjoyable time usually includes a great deal of drinking. At least, that was one thing we never had to worry about with Uncle Sylvester."

"Oh, he never would have thought of doing such a thing," Clarissa cried, but her cousin retorted,

"Of course he would not, for that would have cost money, and Uncle Sylvester would not have spent a penny for drink – or for any other form of enjoyment. But what I meant to say was that the pair of us *are* going to spend a great deal of money and enjoy the very best of everything that London can offer us."

"But London. Oh, we cannot."

It seemed to Clarissa that she had been saying, "we cannot," almost every day of the eight years since she had come to live in the same house with Ariel. Her protests had never stopped Ariel from doing exactly as she pleased and she knew she would follow her cousin's lead this time, as she had always done. Arguments were wasted; still, she ventured a last one.

"What will Henry say?"

Ariel wrinkled her nose slightly as she considered the question. Henry Drayling was the neighbor whose farm marched with Sylvester's acres. He was a worthy young man, but certainly a dull one; sometimes

13

she thought he might have been twenty years her senior, instead of merely two. She had known for more than two years that he hoped some day to win her uncle's consent to their marriage. Of course he had never spoken to her upon the subject. Henry was far too proper – too lacking in dash, Ariel thought – to have approached her without her uncle's permission.

She had often wondered if she truly wanted to marry him. There must be more exciting gentlemen in the world than Henry, although she knew of none. If it had been Sylvester's wish for her to marry Henry, she knew that she would have been given no choice in the matter, since Sylvester was her guardian. She thought sometimes that it might be better than the life she had been leading.

However, her uncle had not seemed to favor the idea of her marriage and now that she had discovered how he had disobeyed the instructions in Lord Watling's will, she was certain that his consent would never have been forthcoming. Upon her marriage, control of her money would have passed into her husband's hands and Sylvester would never have allowed that to happen. Not only would there have been a chance – almost a certainty – that Ariel and her husband might have spent some of the money foolishly, but

14

Sylvester would have had to begin paying for his own expenses and Clarissa's.

"Henry will not like the idea of my going away, I suppose," she admitted. "But I am certain that I can bring him around my thumb."

The first part of her statement was undeniably true; the second was less easy to accomplish. Henry's first impulse upon being told of her scheme was to forbid her to go, but he restrained himself. His years of acquaintance with Ariel made him certain that such action would only make her more determined to have her way. It would be much wiser to use a softer approach with her.

"I had thought –" he began. "You have known that I cared for you for some time – I had intended – and you will need someone to take care of you –"

"But it is too soon."

Ariel could visualize her life with Henry. Perhaps it would be a bit better than with Sylvester, because she did not think Henry would be so stingy. But would there be much difference after all? She could imagine the same dull round of days. Henry had always been a good but unexciting friend, but she did not think that she loved him.

She looked at him now, his round face with pale blue eyes – and his hair. Was it truly

15

beginning to thin at twenty, or had it always been so scant? He would be bald before he was thirty. No, she was certain that she did not love him.

Ariel had no thought of going to London in search of a husband, but one tiny corner of her mind whispered that she *might* meet someone there who was impossible to resist. If no such person appeared, she had no doubt that she would come back and marry Henry eventually. In the meantime, she wanted a bit of the excitement which she felt had been lacking in her life until now.

"It would be a very quiet ceremony," Henry argued, thinking, of course, that she had meant it was too soon after her uncle's death. "In your situation, with no other kin, people will understand why we do not wait. You ought not to be alone."

"I am not alone. I have Clare."

"That was not what I meant," he said patiently, wondering why one who was usually so clever as Ariel could fail to understand a matter as simple as this. "You ought to have a man to take care of you. As for Clarissa, she can come to us, of course, until she decides to marry."

He was already seeing the improvements which he could make upon the two estates, for, lacking other heirs, Mr. Morwin's

16

property would certainly descend to his two nieces. Everyone was aware that Morwin had always been such a nip-farthing that he had not made the necessary repairs upon his place as a concerned owner would have done.

It would take some money to put it into proper shape, but it was a good piece of property and they would have the money they needed to make those improvements. He might even be able to tile that field of his which was in need of drainage.

Henry's great passion was for the land, but he had always been as fond of Ariel as it was possible for him to be of anyone. Her black hair, brown eyes, and vivid coloring were more to his taste than was her cousin's pale prettiness. He would have taken Clarissa, if necessary, to obtain the land, but Clarissa did not have the money for the necessary improvements.

Despite Sylvester's attempts to keep the matter quiet, Henry had learned that Ariel had an income from her father's estate and he had seen at once how it could be put to use on his farm. It had been a pleasant surprise to discover that she was the possessor not merely of a competence, but of a fortune.

He could see nothing amiss in his plans for appropriating Ariel's inheritance for building up the property. After all, the law declared that a wife's money belonged to her husband, and what better way to use it than in improving their land? If there was as much money as had been rumored, he might even be able to buy several of the neighboring farms. He could think of two or three which would be much better with a concerned man in charge of them.

"I would have to hire more men to handle the work," he said to himself, "but I would be careful to get those who could be trusted to improve the land."

It was true that a part of Morwin's estate belonged to Ariel's cousin, but he was willing that a modest sum – no more than was necessary to provide her with a husband as quickly as possible and take her off their hands – should be set aside for her dowry in place of the acres which he coveted as greedily as he coveted Ariel – or more properly, Ariel's fortune.

So certain had he been of success that it came as something of a shock to hear Ariel say firmly, "No, Henry, there will be no talk of our marrying until I have returned from my visit to London."

Henry argued the point at some length; neither he nor any of their neighbors had ever gone to London, so why should there be anything in the city which could appeal to the

18

girl? All of their modest needs could be filled either from the farm or in the village. The only reason he could understand for traveling was to purchase more stock.

Ariel, however, was unyielding.

"I have never been farther away from this estate than to the village since I came here to live with Uncle Sylvester, and neither has Clare. There must be other things to be seen, and I am determined that we shall see London." And that London shall see us as well, she thought, but did not say, for Henry would not understand what she meant.

"If you care so much to see London, I could take you there later," he offered. "But just now – the lambs –"

Later, he thought, if she had not got this maggot of visiting London out of her head, he could argue the plowing or the harvesting for further postponement of the trip. Once they were married, and especially when she had children to care for, Ariel would forget all this foolish desire to be on the gad, spending money which could be put to better use on their property. Or if she had not forgotten it, he could see that she did not have the money for the journey.

Having known Henry for the greater part of her life, Ariel had a very good idea of the thoughts which were filling his mind at the moment. If he truly wished to accompany her to London, there was no reason why he could not do so at this time. She was well aware that all of the lambs were of a size that they could be left for a time. He must think her very green to offer so thin an excuse.

At any rate, she did not wish a trip to London with Henry, at least not this first trip. He would object to all of the things which she was planning to do. Most of all, she knew he would object to the great amount of money which she intended to spend. One man had kept her in unnecessary poverty for the greater part of her life; for the present, she had no intention of allowing another to do the same.

Stubbornly, she shook her head to all of his arguments and repeated her determination to go. At last Henry admitted defeat.

"Very well, have your trip, if that is what you think you must do," he said with the air of one who was conferring a great favor. "I cannot understand why it should be so important to you and I doubt that you'll find much to do there, since both of you will be in mourning. Still, I suppose that you can see a few of the sights, if it means so much to you to do so. But why should you want to visit a dirty, noisy place when you have everything you need right here?"

"I cannot explain it, I know," Ariel said, tempted to ask him how he could know whether or not it was a dirty, noisy place, since neither he nor anyone he knew had ever visited the city. Henry; however, did not like it when she quizzed him. And he would not understand if she tried to explain that *she* could not find everything she needed here. "Still, I intend to go."

A week or two of sightseeing should be enough for her, he thought; nonetheless, he decided to be generous.

"If you stay longer than a month, however, I warn you that I shall come and bring you home."

"But how can you leave the poor lambs?" Ariel asked innocently and Henry had the grace to color slightly. He had never liked the levity which Ariel was all too prone to display upon occasion, but once they were married, she would settle down as she ought. He would see that she did so. Bidding her farewell, he repeated his promise to come for her if she did not return within the promised month.

TWO

Ariel breathed a sigh of relief when she was alone and went off to tell Clarissa the results of their interview. Disappointed that Henry's arguments had proved no more effective than her own, for she was more frightened than she would admit to her daring cousin at the thought of such an enormous place as London, Clarissa agreed that a month should certainly be enough for them to see all the sights of the city.

This remark made Ariel shout with laughter.

"Clare, my sweet goose. A month will not be nearly enough time for all of the things I plan to do. And I have not the slightest intention of returning in so short a time, no matter what Henry may say about it. He is not my master yet, and I am not certain whether or not he ever will be."

"You know that he will be angry –"

"Well, he should know better than to try to give me orders. If he continues to behave in such a manner, he will never have this property, which I know is his true reason for wanting our marriage."

22

"Oh no. I am certain that he loves you."

"Have you never wondered how well he would love me if I had not property and no money?"

Clarissa shook her head and her cousin grimaced as she admitted, "Well, I have. But then I am not as kind as you, Clare. And no matter what Henry thinks, I can tell you that we are going to do much more in London than merely wander about looking at a few of the sights. We are going to *be* seen as well. The first thing we shall do is to find the best dressmakers in the city and have them make us dozens of the most beautiful and dashing outfits possible. Then we shall hire a house and give grand balls and –"

"Ariel, this is not right. How can you think of such things, and so soon after Uncle Sylvester's death?"

"I cannot feel that we owe anything to Uncle Sylvester's memory, Clare. You will say that he took care of the pair of us; that is true enough, if you can call it taking care to make drudges out of us. It was bad enough when we thought we were earning our keep, but now it develops that he supported himself as well as both of us on *my* money for the past thirteen years – and this is what we had in return."

A sweeping gesture indicated all the

23

disagreeable tasks which had fallen to their lot.

"Would he have taken us in at all if he had to bear the expense of our upkeep? You may believe that he would have, but *I* think he would have left us both at the nearest orphanage. And when I remember that he did not tell me that I became mistress of my fortune on my last birthday, I can only wonder how long he would have kept that information from me if he had lived."

Clarissa would have liked to speak up in defense of Sylvester, but she knew that anything she might say would be useless. Every condemning statement Ariel had made about him was the truth. His generosity in taking them in, to which their uncle had referred every time he refused to allow something they wished, had been nothing of the sort.

As for the proposed trip to London, Clarissa might not think it the right thing to do at this time, but if Henry had not been able to persuade Ariel to give over such a madcap scheme, how could *she* hope to do so? She had never been able to influence her cousin in the slightest. However, little as she might know about the outside world, there was one thing she did know, and she made the last attempt.

"But how can you – how can we go to

London by ourselves? We must have a chaperon."

"A single female would not be able to go without one, certainly. But no one will raise an eyebrow if a widow has only her dear cousin for companionship. That is why I plan to go as a widow."

She was not at all certain that this was true, but she stated it so positively that her dear cousin could not doubt her.

Clarissa sighed and gave over trying to change Ariel's mind. Daunted though she might be at the thought of London, she was secretly more than a bit curious about the city, for the girls had spoken of it often as they went about their work, spinning tales about it as they might about any unattainable place.

Still, the thought of actually leaving home and traveling to so large a place was a frightening one. If Ariel were to travel with Henry to protect her – as her husband, of course – that would be quite a different matter. Ariel might be convinced that she could care for herself, but in Clarissa's mind, a gentleman *was* actually necessary to take care of such things as horses and bills, and those mysterious things called posting charges.

Ariel had refused to purchase mourning clothing, saying that their own dark gowns would serve the purpose well enough until they left home. Being only a bit more than a year old, they were much less worn than those they had frequently been forced to wear and the villagers would not expect them to spend any money on clothing, being unaware that Lady Ariel was actually a very wealthy woman. Her uncle's clutch-fisted ways had led his acquaintances to believe that the household lived in the most straitened circumstances

"We could not buy new gowns here unless they *were* mourning," she declared. "And we shall certainly not wear it when we get to London. I refuse to do so and I forbid you to wear it, either."

Preparing for their journey was a simpler matter. Henry had agreed to look after the estate for them, for he considered that it would belong to him as soon as Ariel returned from London, and the girls had no more than the barest necessities of clothing to pack.

They had discovered in the attic an old trunk which had belonged to Ariel's father and which his brother-in-law had kept because he had been unable to find a buyer for it. One corner had been broken, but the damage was not great; and when the dust had been cleared from it, the girls discovered that it bore the Watling crest.

"Old as it is, it is almost too fine for our rags," Ariel said looking at the few things which Clarissa was folding with her customary neatness. All their possessions were not enough to fill the trunk, so Ariel fetched some old books which had belonged to her father and whose sadly worn condition had made it impossible for Sylvester to sell them.

There had been more of them, but one day Sylvester had taken the ones the girls were reading and had burned them to save fuel, so his niece had quickly hidden these. They and the broken trunk were all that she had which had belonged to her father.

Their packing done, they loaded the trunk into the rickety gig and hitched up the poor old horse which their uncle had used for his occasional trips from home.

"At the very first posting house we come to, I am going to see if I can *buy* a better horse," declared Ariel, as ignorant of the ways of the road as her cousin, but determined not to admit it.

She only hoped that this ancient animal would last until they could reach a spot where a younger one might be purchased. They had discovered nearly one hundred guineas tucked away in various spots in Sylvester's desks and cabinets – most of it garnered, although they did not know it, a bit at a time from Ariel's income during the years she had lived with him – and this would certainly last them until they reached London and laid claim to Ariel's inheritance.

The horse's best speed was a slow walk and both girls pitied it too much to try to urge it to go faster. It was fortunate that, only a mile or two beyond the village, a horse fair was being held that day. Dismayed by the rough appearance of many of the men who thronged the grounds, Clarissa clutched at her cousin's arm and begged her to go on, but Ariel turned the gig toward the crowd, saying,

"We shall never arrive in London at this rate. We *must* have something better to drive than this."

Shocked though most of them might be at the thought of two young females approaching them with the thought of purchasing a horse, several of the dealers were able to overcome their feelings far enough to offer their stock, only to discover that the dark-haired female was far more knowledgeable than they would have expected her to be, for Henry had taught Ariel a great deal about horses, thinking that, when they were married, she might care for the stock while he tended his acres.

After curtly dismissing several showy offerings whose wind she would not have depended upon to last until the next toll gate

28

was reached, Ariel found one dealer willing to sell her a prime young animal, only asking her about twice its worth.

Although she was aware that she was being cheated, Ariel paid the price without haggling because Clarissa was becoming so disturbed by the leers and comments of some of the rougher men that she continued to tug at her cousin's arm and beg her to come away. The dealer generously offered to take the old horse off their hands, allowing them fully one tenth of what he would expect to get for him from some other customer, and the pair resumed their journey, greatly to Clarissa's relief.

Ariel's self-confidence was puffed up by this evidence that she could manage for herself upon the road, but it received a severe shock when the two stopped at a posting house for the night.

It was true that the two girls did not make a grand appearance in their outmoded gowns, but the house itself was a small one, which could scarcely expect to attract many important guests. It scarcely seemed that their appearance was enough to account for the sneer in the landlord's tone when he told them that he had no room. This despite the fact that the stables were occupied by a single team of magnificent chestnuts, proof that there could be only one or two other persons in the house.

Never having been permitted to travel, Ariel was unaware of the suspicion with which managers of respectable establishments were wont to view females who arrived without either escorts or servants. It could only be the fact that they looked like a pair of waifs, she thought, which accounted for his hostile attitude. Perhaps he feared that they would prove to be without funds.

"We are well able to pay for our lodgings," she assured him, prepared to show him some of the money if it was necessary, but the man only said,

"Aye, I have no doubt that you are – but you'll not have the chance to earn more beneath my roof."

So that was the problem! He thought that they had come in search of employment, doubtless as chambermaids. Silently, she heaped maledictions upon Sylvester and his pennypinching ways. Why could he not have provided them with clothing which was more suited to their stations, instead of dressing them like servants?

She could see now that it would have been wiser to have insisted upon taking the time to purchase new gowns before they started upon their journey. Anything which they could have found in the village would certainly have been outmoded by London standards, but there was not a doubt that it would have been better than what they were now wearing. However, with no way of knowing what expenses they might incur along the way, she had thought it would be best to save their money for the trip itself.

"You misunderstand," she said with more patience than was customary for her, since she could understand that it was not entirely the man's fault that he had misjudged them. "I am Lady Ariel Laurence and this is my cousin, Miss Morwin. We have stopped here for a night's lodging on our way to London; we have no need to seek employment."

"Lady, is it?" the landlord sneered. "Ladybird would be more the way of it."

"Hold, Raskin," came a lazy voice. "You must permit me to stand surety for her ladyship."

Both of the girls turned to stare at the figure which was seated near the fire, positive that they could never have seen him before, for who could easily forget so elegant a person as he? That he was someone of importance, above the type of guest which one might ordinarily expect in a house of this size, was made clear by the sudden change in the landlord's manner toward the girls.

"Of course," he said, bowing very low to the pair of them. "I must beg your ladyship's

31

pardon for not having recognized you the moment you entered, and I can only hope that you will be kind enough to overlook what I said. Sally will be here on the instant to conduct you to your bedchamber and you have only to ask for whatever you wish. The best room for these two ladies. At once, Sally."

"But – but the gentleman's things are already in that room," Sally faltered.

"Then have them moved," the gentleman ordered, and, although Ariel protested such action, the landlord seconded the order, assuring the young ladies that only the best would do for them.

Ariel nodded a cool acceptance of his sudden deference and looked toward the stranger, saying, "We owe you our deep thanks, sir, for having come to our assistance and for giving up your room, although that was not necessary. We could easily have taken another."

The gentleman rose and came toward them. With only Sylvester and the neighbors to which she could compare him, Ariel was unaccustomed to the niceties of a gentleman's dress, but she could not fail to be aware of how well his gray coat and buckskins fitted his tall, well-built frame, or how brightly his boots gleamed in the firelight.

The light also glinted upon his burnished dark red hair as he took her hand and bowed low over it. When he straightened, she could see that his eyes were an unusual colour– in fact, she thought of them as amber, like the eyes of some animal – and there was a light in them which sent an odd feeling through her.

"I would not wish anyone to say," the gentleman told her in that same lazy tone, "that Dexter had ever been remiss in his attentions to a lady. I trust that your ladyship will rest well."

There was something in the smile he gave her which made Ariel feel that his words carried some meaning other than she had understood. Somewhat confused, she curtsied slightly and turned to follow the serving girl up the stairs, Clarissa upon her heels.

Below them, they could hear the landlord break into excited speech. His words were unclear, but there was no doubt that his tone was one of apology. The stranger, however, was much nearer to the stairway and his words came to them plainly.

"Quality, Raskin? Certainly not. You were not taken in for a moment by their story, were you?"

Raskin spoke again, this time with considerable heat, and his lordship laughed.

"Nothing of that sort, you may be sure. I think it far more likely that they are a pair of lady's maids, who have borrowed their mistress' name for a visit to the city. It is unfortunate that they were not able to borrow her clothing as well, for she certainly did not provide well for them. I thought it would be a pity to spoil their little masquerade. You need not fear that they will damage the reputation of your house."

Again there was the sound of the landlord's voice. He appeared to be protesting against the trick which had been played upon him and at the same time attempting to show that he did not hold the gentleman to blame for his part in it.

"I can assure you," the stranger said, still with laughter in his voice, "that these two *must* be virtuous. I have had experience enough, although you might not know it, to be able to tell you that no drab would allow herself to be seen in such a get-up as that. If those two young females are guilty of anything, it must be of robbing a dustbin for their clothing. Still, I must admit that the black-haired one is a very pretty piece."

Ariel gasped, uncertain whether she ought to be more angered by the stranger's disparagement of their clothing – it was certainly deserving of scorn, but it was not his place to say so – or of being called a "pretty piece," which sounded insulting.

She half turned about, with the intention of going downstairs and putting him properly in his place, but Clarissa, remembering how narrowly they had escaped being refused shelter, pushed her farther up the stairs and she allowed herself to be guided to their room.

THREE

Having learned from Sally that the posting house was not large enough to boast a private dining room and fearing that her cousin's quick temper might lead her to make some remarks to Lord Dexter which might be unbecoming – especially after he had been kind enough to vouch for them and to give up his room – Clarissa pleaded her fatigue, which was real enough, as an excuse for not wishing to go down to dinner. She begged Ariel not to leave her.

"I think it would be best if I should rest now," she argued, "and it would be unthinkable for you to dine alone belowstairs, for you might have to share the gentleman's table."

Being unaccustomed to driving for a great distance, and having the additional task of managing the horse, Ariel was truthfully almost as fatigued as her cousin. Her great concern, however, was for Clarissa, for the younger girl had always been inclined to be a bit delicate. She agreed that it might be better if they had dinner in their rooms, if that might be arranged.

Fearful of being thought as great a clutch-fist as her uncle had been, Ariel rewarded Sally so handsomely for the extra service that the girl gladly struggled up the stairs with trays of food, convinced that despite their garments, which were of much poorer quality then anything she possessed, these guests were indeed ladies.

Although he had been quick to describe the two young females as little imposters, but certainly virtuous, the gentleman with the red hair would not have been averse to whiling away an hour or two in dalliance with either of them, had they shown the slightest inclination to oblige him in this manner for his courtesy to them. His preference would have been for the dark-haired one, for he admired her impudence in claiming to be a member of the Quality, and he thought that she had much more spirit than the other.

He had already learned that the inn was

rather lacking in female company and had looked forward to seeing the young pair again. However, since they did not come downstairs at dinnertime, he assumed that they might truly be as virtuous as he had assured the landlord they were and therefore unworthy of his further interest. He had already discovered that Sally had no such scruples.

Dismissing the others from his mind, he went on his way early the next morning and they did not see him again – to Clarissa's great relief and to Ariel's vague disappointment.

Upon reflection, she had convinced herself that he had not intended to insult her by referring to her as a "pretty piece." Doubtless that was merely the manner in which London gentlemen expressed their approval of a lady, and she was forced to admit that he was quite the handsomest gentleman who had crossed her limited sphere, so it was pleasant to think that he considered her pretty. If he had seemed a trifle arrogant, surely a nobleman had a right to behave in such a manner.

She was slightly sorry that she had not overruled Clare and insisted upon their descending to the dining room. His lordship would have been there and she could have begun by thanking him again for coming to their assistance and for giving up his room. Then, if he had appeared to be willing to talk, she could have asked him some questions about London.

Still, we shall soon be able to see everything for ourselves, she reflected, so there is no longer any need to have someone to tell us about it, and dismissed the gentleman from her mind for the more important business of reaching the city.

Sally had confided to them that while the inn did not often cater to members of Quality, she had heard those who did stay mention Grillon's Hotel in the city. The cousins gave her their thanks and another golden present from Ariel and went on their way, grateful for the name of a respectable establishment. In so large a place as London, there must be a number of hotels and it would have proven embarrassing if they had stumbled into one of lesser repute.

However, Sally had not been able to tell them in what part of the city the hotel might be located and they were forced to ask directions after they reached London. Several of the persons they questioned merely looked at them and sneered, one or two of the gentlemen had made improper suggestions, and one was so determined to enter the gig with them that Ariel was forced to use her whip to drive him off. Others were more polite and sent them farther along each time they became lost, so that the hotel was finally reached.

The staff at the hotel was too well accustomed to the vagaries of the Quality to see anything amiss when Lady Ariel Laurence arrived at their door accompanied only by another young lady. The very shabbiness of the pair was proof, as it had been to Lord Dexter, that these were not members of the frail sisterhood, and the golden guineas that her ladyship gave out assured them of excellent accommodations.

The gig had acquired some comment among the ostlers at the stable where it was left – although not in the ladies' hearing – and Ariel was aware of some of the curious stares which had been aimed at their old gowns.

"The first thing we shall do tomorrow morning," she said decidedly to Clarissa, "is to pay a call upon Mr. MacPherson, who handled my father's affairs, and get a great deal of money. *Then* we shall make the rounds of all the best dressmakers and milliners. Being thought a dowd is becoming quite wearisome."

Clarissa nodded agreement, for she knew that Ariel would do as she said, no matter what her cousin thought. Privately, the younger girl did not consider that their appearance was so *very* bad. It was true that her gown was becoming a bit tight for, unlike Ariel, she had not yet attained her full growth at the time it had been made and she found that the manner in which it displayed her bosom was a bit embarrassing. She knew nothing at all of London fashions, except for some of the people they had seen upon their way to the hotel, and their modes differed greatly, depending upon where they had been seen. Ariel, however, knew no more than she, so how could she be certain that they were dressed unfashionably? Also, Clarissa could not help thinking that it was not proper for them to forget Uncle Sylvester so soon.

The next morning, they learned that a hackney could be summoned to convey them to Mr. MacPherson's offices. Ariel was unwilling to admit that she had found the traffic of London's busy streets and the unpleasantness they had encountered from some of those whom they had asked for directions almost as frightening as Clarissa had done, so she merely declared that she would not drive again until she had purchased a more fashionable vehicle than the old gig.

In the office of the firm, they were met at first by an ancient clerk who managed, without uttering a word, to convey his disapproval of females who would visit a place of business, and especially of females who looked as these two did. He unbent a trifle upon being presented with the letters which had been signed by his employer and conducted them to Mr. MacPherson's sanctum.

The young man who was seated behind the large desk glanced up from the papers he had been examining when they were announced. Leaping to his feet, he knocked over his chair and caught his inkwell barely in time to prevent it from spilling its contents across a stack of important documents. He was as startled as the clerk had been by the arrival of ladies – and especially such ladies as these.

Most people would find the dark-haired one striking, he supposed, but his gaze had passed over her and had fastened almost at once upon the second lady's face. If the young man had ever been required to describe his ideal woman, he would have been at a loss for words, but he knew in this instant that he had found her.

Pale gold curls clustered softly about a face whose natural beauty was enhanced by the rosy blush which spread over it as she became aware of his admiring gaze. Seldom had he seen eyes of so beautiful a shade of blue, he thought, as she looked away, then glanced shyly back to see that he was still staring at her. And had any other woman in the world a

mouth so softly curved, so sweetly tinted, so –
so kissable?

Dimly aware that the other lady had said
something to him, he reluctantly withdrew his
gaze from the vision and gave her companion
an enquiring look.

"Mr. MacPherson?" Ariel asked again,
unaccustomed to being overlooked, but
somewhat amused at the attention he was
paying to her cousin. When they were alone,
she would quiz Clare about her conquest, but
she would do so gently, for the child had a
great deal of sensibility and Ariel did not wish
that she should be hurt.

"Y-yes – I am James MacPherson." He
found it hard to concentrate upon what he
was saying.

"Nonsense. You cannot be," the angel's
companion said sharply.

It was one thing, Ariel thought, for him to
be dazzled by Clare; to claim that he had
been Archibald Laurence's man of business
was another thing entirely. He might be one
and twenty years of age, but certainly no
more than that, a slim young man of no
more than medium height, with light brown
hair and eyes which appeared more green than
blue. Doubtless, he was nothing more than an
office boy who had been sent in here to look
for some papers his employer wished.

"You are not old enough," she told him. "I know that Mr. MacPherson was my father's friend as well as the man who handled his affairs. And he – my father – has been dead these thirteen years."

"Oh." He understood now what was troubling her. "You must be speaking of *my* father. He is also James MacPherson – or it would be more accurate to say that I am also James MacPherson, since, of course, it was I who was named after him. My father is out of the city at present, but perhaps I may be of service to you in his absence."

"That explains it."

The lady's tone was quite different; in fact, Ariel was thinking that she had behaved foolishly, not an unusual state for her. Why must she always speak without thinking? She had known that the company was known as MacPherson and Son, but she believed it to be an old firm and had supposed that the son would prove to be the man who had been her father's friend.

"I trust you will pardon me for what I said," she went on. "I must confess that I am unaccustomed to handling matters of business."

"No apologies are called for, madam," James MacPherson assured her. "It is seldom that one meets a lady who *does* know anything of business."

"Oh, I see. Then perhaps it was not the right thing for me to have come here. But there is no one else who could handle these matters for me. I am Lady Ariel Laurence and this is my cousin, Miss Morwin. But of course, you will wish proof of my identity."

She drew from her reticule the same papers which had already been examined by the elderly clerk and offered them to him.

"Here is the correspondence which my uncle exchanged with your office and the letter I received from your father after he had been informed of my uncle's death. Also, several other papers which should prove that I am who I say I am."

The thought came into James' mind that no one accompanied by such an angel could possibly be other than honest, but he refrained from uttering it. He could almost hear the scorn his father would pour upon him should he hear of such unprofessional dealings. Instead, he took the papers, read the last letter carefully, then excused himself to bring the box containing the records of the Laurence account.

As a junior partner of the firm, it would have been well within his province to have ordered one of the clerks to fetch it, but both

44

of them were old men – one had worked under his grandfather – and they were inclined to look doubtful and even to argue whenever "Master Jamie" required something of them. He had no desire to be made to look so foolish before the lovely Miss Morwin – or before her ladyship, for that matter.

He returned to the desk, dropping the box in his confusion when he realized that he had neglected to invite the ladies to be seated. Repairing this omission with many apologies, he retrieved the box and took refuge behind his desk to look at the more recent papers which dealt with the account.

More than a little puzzled by the information he gleaned, for this was not one of the accounts which had previously passed through his hands, he said, "Lady Ariel, I see that, before the letter you showed me, my father had written to you several times since your last birthday, but had received no reply from you, only from Mr. Morwin. I understand that he was your guardian."

"That is true – my uncle. I never received the earlier letters or was told of them. We found them among his papers after he died. Although I could not find any copy of his correspondence, for he would doubtless have thought keeping a copy was a waste of paper, I believe that you may find that he had arranged with your father to continue paying the income as before, for that appears to be all he received. Until I read the letters, I had no idea that the control of my father's money should have come to me or that it amounted to so much."

This remark shocked Mr. MacPherson, and he re-examined the papers in search of any evidence that Mr. Morwin had been cheating his niece. At last he said, "Yes, he requested that only the income be paid to you and it does not seem that he has ever drawn any sums of money for his own use. The bank has sent us only records of the usual payments having been forwarded to him, which would fit with your thought of what had occurred."

"Yes." Angry though she might have been with Sylvester for having kept the knowledge of her fortune from her, Ariel was forced to be fair to his memory. "I know that my uncle would never have tried to take my fortune. He did not tell me only because Uncle Sylvester did not believe in spending money. As anyone can tell you looking at the pair of us."

His attention being called to the fact, the young man became aware that the ladies were not clad in the height of fashion – far from it, in fact. Not that the latest modes or the finest fabrics could be considered necessary to enhance the appearance of the lovely Miss

46

Morwin – she would look beautiful no matter what she was wearing. He supposed that the same might be said of Lady Ariel.

However, having a desire to ape several of the styles which were set by the dandies, a desire which was thwarted both by his father's orders and by the shortness of funds at his disposal – he could sympathize with their wish to be fashionable.

Attempting to assure them that it did not matter in the least what they wore, he floundered amid a confusion of half-completed sentences, growing redder and more embarrassed with each phrase, while Clarissa blushed with him and wished that she could help him. At last Ariel took pity on the young man and said,

"Pray do not concern yourself with trying to flatter us, Mr. MacPherson. It is a waste of your time. We are well aware that we look like dairy maids – and unsuccessful ones at that. Our first concern is to have the matter of our wardrobes put to rights. But, being a gentleman, I do not suppose you would know where we should begin."

Young Mr. MacPherson had never had any desire to provide wearables for a member of the muslin company – a fortunate thing, for he would not have had the funds to do so – but he had heard enough from family and

47

friends to be able to stammer that he believed that the best fashions were to be found in Bond Street.

Then, remembering a spirited family discussion at the time his eldest cousin was being prepared for her come-out, he added, "I have heard that Madame Josette is considered to be one of the best. But I think that she is quite expensive."

"Must I worry about the expense?"

"Certainly not, Lady Ariel; you will be able to spend whatever you wish."

"Then we shall certainly call upon Madame Josette, for that is precisely what we wish, is it not, Clare?"

Clarissa murmured something which might have been taken for agreement, although privately she could not understand why a gown should cost a great deal. Cloth was not expensive – at least the sort of cloth they were accustomed to use – and the girls had always made their own. Sylvester had insisted that they should be made with no waste of cloth beyond the allowance which was made for them to grow into the garments, and of course, with no trimming.

Still, with the young gentleman's gaze returning to her at intervals, she thought for the first time that it might be nice to have one *pretty* gown even if it should cost as much as a pound. Ariel was so generous; she would not begrudge the expense, Clarissa knew.

"Of course, all of this will take money, a great deal of money, since we have nothing fit to wear in London," Ariel was saying. "Can you let us have it or must you give us a letter to the bank – Hoare's bank, I believe it is – so that they will let us have what we need?"

"Oh no." Mr. MacPherson was shocked at the suggestion, but made a quick recover to say, "It is not the custom, that is, not in London, for ladies to deal with banks. You will have your bills sent to us, of course. There is no need for you to concern yourself with such matters."

"That will be very nice. I assure you that there will be a great many bills for, as I told you, we lack everything; and I am certain that we shall also want many things which we do not truly need. But we shall need money as well for – oh, for many things."

She would not admit how greatly she longed to have money in her hands to spend as she pleased after so many years of having Uncle Sylvester grudge every penny which was necessary for their living, even though it had not come from his pocket.

"That will be no problem. I shall be happy to get what you need and to bring it to you."

This was another task which might well

have been left to one of the company's clerks, but James thought that if he obtained the money and took it to them himself, it would give him another opportunity to see Miss Morwin – perhaps even to exchange a few words with her, which he had not been able to do at present. "Where are you staying?"

"At Grillon's Hotel – but only for the present. I think that we ought to have a house, but we arrived in the city only yesterday and have not yet had time to search for one."

"I shall be happy to take care of that matter for you, as well," Mr. MacPherson assured her.

He was certain that his father would be only too pleased to have him spend whatever time was necessary in the service of so important a client as Lady Ariel Laurence, although, as far as the young gentleman was concerned, Lady Ariel was merely the cousin of the angel.

"Have you planned to purchase a house or to hire one?"

"I think it might be the best thing if I should hire one – that is, if I can find something we like. We may wish to travel later on."

She caught Clarissa's surprised look at this and gave her an impish grin. How important it made one feel to discuss such matters as this, knowing that it was not necessary to give a thought to the cost. With almost unlimited funds at her disposal, Ariel was in much the same position as a greedy child suddenly turned loose in a sweet shop; she wanted everything she saw.

"And I decide that I should like to travel," she went on. "I do not know if I wish a permanent residence in London. But whether we buy or hire, we shall wish a place which is large enough for us to entertain a great many people – when we have made some friends."

"I understand that, certainly. If you wish to hire, I know of a place which you might like, completely furnished and staffed."

The son of a former client of the firm, whose predilection for betting upon all the wrong things, whether horses or cards, plus his taste for the most expensive of mistresses, had driven him so far into dun territory that he could never hope to make a recovery, especially if left to his own devices, had finally been forced to retire to the country to escape his creditors.

The family house in London was now vacant, the baronet's widowed mother having gone sometime earlier to live with her daughter where she need not be plagued by demands that *she* settle some of her son's debts – which she could scarcely have done, since he had already talked her into turning over to him most of her assets and they had followed his own. Although the hire of the house would not rescue the young nobleman, it might allay the most impatient of his creditors for a time.

"It is located in Cavendish Square," James explained.

"Is that a good location?" Ariel disliked the necessity of admitting to such ignorance of the city, but this young man already knew her as a country mouse so it would not matter.

"An excellent one," he assured her with a smile. "And you may see it whenever you wish. I think you will find it suitable for any entertaining you may wish to do. Of course, if it does not please you, we can easily find something else."

"I should like to see it, but it must wait for tomorrow, I think. Our first duty is to see Madame Josette and to purchase as many gowns and bonnets and – and other things – as we can."

As she rose to take her leave, Mr. MacPherson, struck by a sudden thought, said, "One moment, Lady Ariel, if you please."

He caught up a paper and pen, threatening the safety of the inkwell again, and hurriedly wrote something.

"This may save you embarrassment, until

you are better known," he said, giving it to Ariel.

On the paper, which was emblazoned with the company's seal, he had written, "The bills for any purchases made by the bearer, Lady Ariel Laurence, will be honored by MacPherson and Son and should be sent to them for payment."

He had signed it, "James MacPherson," copying his father's writing as best he could, certain that the signature of the head of the firm would carry more weight than that of a junior partner, even though the junior partner was a son.

He had a hackney summoned for them and saw them into it personally. When they had thanked him, Ariel hiding her amusement at the thought that none of this concern was on her account, and Clarissa giving him a shy murmur and a smile, he returned to his desk and sat back, trying to think of other ways he could be of service, ways which would, of course, bring him into Miss Morwin's presence.

He was so deep in dreams of her that the elder clerk had to remind him three times – finally in the tones he would have used to an errant schoolboy – that another client was waiting to see him. He gave orders at once for the gentleman to be brought in, but it was doubtful that he gave much thought to the business being conducted.

FOUR

Ariel had good reason to be thankful that James MacPherson had thought to present her with the voucher. Without the endorsement of such a well-known firm, it is doubtful that two young ladies in their countrified garb would have been permitted to pass through the doors of Madame Josette's select establishment.

The paper, implying as it did that a considerable expenditure might be made, was enough to bring the famous designer herself out to greet them after one of her assistants had whispered a description, a most disparaging one, of the prospective clients. Certainly, such as they could be persuaded to spend a great deal.

Her personal greeting was a far greater compliment than either of the young ladies could know. Madame's fame was now great enough that she seldom gave individual attention to her customers, no matter how famous they might be. Such a disregard for their importance only made them the more anxious to be seen in one of her creations, for those who gave the greatest thought to their own consequence contrarily admired those who disregarded it.

When her assistant described the two newcomers, Madame found it most difficult to believe, but Miss Tibbs was not given to lying, so she came out to see for herself. The description had not been exaggerated and the couturiere looked at them with something akin to horror, reflecting that she had been better gowned than they when she was plain Josie Pike in Shoreditch.

Seeing her expression and well aware of its cause, Ariel was moved to confide the sort of life they had spent in their uncle's care and Josette, who had grown up with poverty, but never with miserliness, was all sympathy in a moment. Immediately, Ariel and Clarissa found themselves in a small room, surrounded by a host of females, being handled, measured, and completely discussed.

"It will take a little time to outfit you properly," Madame Josette declared. "But let us see what we can do for you at once, for you must not be allowed to go about any longer in what you are now wearing. I have the very thing."

She turned to a young woman who had been hovering at her side and ordered, "Bring out that walking gown that Lady Soames wished for her daughter. It is almost finished and I think it will do very well for her ladyship."

Both girls stared when the item was brought in. Accustomed to their drab-colored gowns, they had not dreamed that anything could be so fine. The vivid green-blue of a peacock's feather, the gown was simply made with only a ruffling of blond lace at the neck and sleeves. As it was slipped over Ariel's head and she turned so that the girl could fasten the many tiny buttons up the back, Clarissa exclaimed,

"Oh Ariel, it is beautiful. You are beautiful."

"Yes, I was right. It is the gown you should have," Madame agreed, nodding to another young woman, who came forward and began pinning here and there to adjust the fit to Ariel's figure, which was slimmer, especially in the waist and hips – than that of the young lady for whom it had been intended.

"You should always wear vivid colors, my dear. With your dark hair and eyes and your lovely skin – your country life has done *that* for you, at least – it would be shameful to force you to appear in the very pale shades which are considered *de rigueur* for a *jeune fille* – a young miss," she explained, seeing that Ariel had not understood her French.

"Oh, but I do not intend to appear as a young miss," Ariel told her. "Everyone is to think that I am a widow, but one who has now put off her mourning and is going about in society. In that way, I can wear whatever may please me and do anything I like – no matter how greatly some people may be shocked."

The couturiere laughed heartily, recognizing a spirit as reckless as her own. "Ah, I see it. You wish to live, to experience every excitement. You will not be hedged in upon all sides like a young girl would be. That is how it should be, I think. How fortunate it is that you decided to come to me."

The gown, now pinned to fit and with the hem let down because of Ariel's greater height, was lifted over her head and borne away for the young woman to complete these necessary alterations. Looking after it, Ariel said, "But did you not say, Madame, that the gown had been intended for someone else?"

Madame's unpretty but expressive face twisted into a grimace.

"One of my assistants foolishly allowed Lady Soames to – how do you say it?" It pleased Josette to pretend an unfamiliarity with the cant terms which had been a part of her daily life. "Ah yes, to bullock her into agreeing that this gown would be suitable for her daughter – which I can tell you, it is not.

I objected the moment I heard of it, but the material had already been cut.

"According to the young lady's instructions, it was – if you can believe it – to be trimmed with yards of floss and dozens of bows. And for one of that size. She would have looked like one of the horses in Astley's Amphitheater. It is also the wrong color for the girl, entirely. I shall tell Lady Soames just that; she will bluster, but what can she do? I shall personally tell her – I, Josette – that the child needs softer colors, also a plain style of gown, without trimmings, for her figure, especially if she continues to indulge in sweets. You are slimmer and have the height to carry it."

"But will she not be angry?"

Madame shrugged. "That may be so, but I shall tell her that if she is not pleased with my decision she is welcome to go elsewhere for her daughter's gowns. The girl will do me no credit, no matter how much attention I give her. But you will see – her ladyship will not go, for where would she? Now, let us see what we can do to bring *la petite mademoiselle* into style."

She took Clarissa by the hand and turned her about, studying her coloring and figure as she had done with Ariel.

"Ah yes, you are the one to wear the soft

colors, the young styles. The bright colors and the daring modes I plan for her ladyship will never do for you, so I hope that you do not plan to copy her. If you do, I shall not dress you, which would be a shame. It will be a pleasure to design your costumes in contrast; each of you will be a perfect foil for the other. But for the moment, what are we to do?"

One of the seamstresses, as small as Clarissa, approached her employer and spoke in a low tone. At Madame's nod of assent, she turned and said to Clarissa,

"If Miss would not mind – I have a gown that Madame permitted me to make for myself. It has not been worn; I have only just finished it."

"Oh, I could not take *your* gown," Clarissa said in distress, but the girl, seeing how she had pleased Josette by making the offer, said, "I can easily make another. Let me show it to you."

The gown she brought out was of a soft cream color, with a row of tiny cherry-colored bows from neck to hem and also upon the sleeves. The two girls were so nearly of a size that the gown might have been made for Clarissa. She smoothed the soft cloth and blushed as she found herself thinking that it would be nice if Mr. MacPherson could see her wearing a gown so fine as this one, instead of the shabby one which had been all she owned. She had not realized quite how ugly it was until she had seen this lovely thing.

"It is perfect for you, dear," Ariel told her. "Will you allow me to pay the girl for it, Madame?"

"Of a certainty," Madame assured her, all graciousness. "But for the work only."

She named a price which seemed reasonable, even to these country girls. She had originally made the girl a present of the cloth, which had not been quite enough to make up a gown for most of her clients who wanted more ruffles and frills. She intended, moreover, to add not only the cost of that cloth, but the cost of another gown for the shop girl, to Lady Ariel's account. Since her ladyship had not inquired as to the cost of the gowns, she would not notice the additional expense.

There was enough left of the money which the cousins had found among Sylvester's belongings to pay the girl and also to cover the cost of the hackney for their return journey. The pair then spent several delightful hours with Madame Josette, choosing materials and patterns for other gowns. Both of them were quite dazzled by the bolts of cloth Madame ordered out for their inspection – muslins embroidered with tiny flowers, silks, velvets and laces of every hue, sarsenets, both twilled and plain, shimmering cloth woven with threads of gold and silver. How could they ever make a choice among all these wonderful things?

Ariel ordered gown after gown, and Clarissa was moved to protest several times that *she* would not need such a great number, to which her cousin only said with a laugh and a headshake,

"Nonsense. You are to have one for every one that I have. We intend to shine in London society."

"But how can we do that when we do not know anyone here?" Clarrisa thought a bit wistfully of the one person she did know – if only slightly – and thought that one or two new gowns would be enough to impress *him.* And she had a feeling that he was not a part of the society of which Ariel was speaking.

Her question brought a laugh from Madame Josette.

"That is a matter which will soon be remedied, I can tell you," she said. "In all the places you will shop, even among my own assistants, I am certain, there are those who will gossip. Before long the word will be

61

spread that the wealthy Lady Ariel has taken up residence in London."

She intended to discover for herself just how wealthy the lady might actually be before she gave orders to cut into a single piece of the material which the ladies had chosen for their many gowns. Mr. MacPherson's note had said that their bills would be paid, but he might not have been aware of the extent of their purchases.

"You will discover a great number of people who will declare that they certainly must be related to you in some way; if you question them too closely, they will claim that the relationship is unfortunately a distant one, so that you will not be able to prove them wrong. And they will all be anxious to entertain you. Especially if they happen to have sons of marriageable age."

"But we have not come to London to look for husbands," Ariel declared, *almost* certain that they had not done so. Clarissa, entirely certain, shook her head violently.

"Ah, but these ladies who are so anxious to make your acquaintance – they do not need to be told that, do they?" Madame said with another laugh. "You may allow them to make their calls upon you, to invite you to their balls and teas – and if you *should* happen to meet someone you like, so much the better."

Both young ladies laughingly denied that there was any chance of such a thing happening and, since the alterations upon Ariel's gown had been completed, donned their new purchases and departed, while Madame ordered that the castoff clothing be burned. The morning was far gone, so it was decided that they should return to Grillon's Hotel for nuncheon. Here they learned that Mr. MacPherson, misjudging the length of time that females could take in the choice of their gowns, had come and gone.

He had failed in his objective of seeing Miss Morwin again, but he had left a parcel for Lady Ariel and a message that he would call upon the following morning to show the ladies the house in Cavendish Square, if that would prove convenient to them.

The bulky parcel contained a large supply of bank notes and coins and, following the nuncheon to which both girls' country appetites enabled them to do complete justice, they set out for more shopping. Although both of them had stuffed their reticules with money, Ariel planned to continue using James MacPherson's voucher, stifling a giggle as she thought of the enormous number of bills which would, in the next several days, be crossing that gentleman's desk.

It had been his suggestion, of course, that

she should handle her affairs in this manner, but she thought he could not have realized how badly they were in need of all sorts of clothing or what a wonderful feeling it was, after all these years of Uncle Sylvester's clutch-fisted ways, to know that there was money enough to pay for anything she might wish to purchase.

By midafternoon, Clarissa had stopped trying to prevent her cousin from including something for her in every purchase and was reveling in the choice of bonnets, satin slippers, silk stockings, gloves – all the accessories which were necessary to show their new gowns to perfection – as well as a variety of more delicate items. She was not able, however, to restrain her blushes when she viewed the diaphanous nightwear and undergarments which were to replace the chaste home-sewn items they had always worn.

The young ladies took a number of their purchases with them, but instructed the proprietors of the shops to hold the others until they had decided upon a house, for they could imagine the confusion which would occur at Grillon's if such a multitude of parcels were to be delivered there, only to be carried away again within a few days.

Exhausted by their round of shopping,

64

which Ariel declared was only to be the first of many, the pair retired early. The noise of the London traffic, which had interrupted their slumber the night before, could not disturb them now and they did not rise before eight of the clock, an hour which in former days would have been so disgracefully late as to bring down their uncle's wrath. Their guilt at having wasted so much of the day was soon dispelled by the discovery that the hour was unusually early by city standards.

"We shall just have to accustom ourselves to being slugabeds," Ariel said, stretching luxuriously, "for it would seem that here only the servants rise early – and our serving days are over."

They were still enjoying a breakfast which had been large enough to surprise a kitchen staff accustomed to ladies who only picked at their food, when word was brought to them that Mr. MacPherson had arrived. James had determined that he would not miss the ladies this morning, even if it meant that he would have to wait several hours for them to appear, so was delightfully surprised to learn that they were already about and would receive him.

"How eager the young gentleman is," Ariel said when they had given the order to have him brought to them.

"Ariel, please," Clarissa protested, blushing furiously.

"I only meant that he is so eager to have us see the house he has in mind for us," her cousin said mischievously.

"Of – of course." For some reason, the sunshine had quite gone out of the day. Certainly Ariel must be right, his only reason for arriving so promptly was to show the house. He was almost a stranger to them, so what other reason could there have been?

Then he was beside them, imperiling a small table and several chairs as he hurried across the room, reminding Ariel very much of the gamboling of an overgrown puppy. As he bade them good morning, his eyes met Clarissa's and the day was golden again.

She looked away quickly, fervently wishing that she did not blush at the sight or even the thought of the gentleman; how countrified he must think her to behave in such a fashion. Still, she was happy that she was wearing her pretty new gown this morning, unaware that, aside from thinking that she was more beautiful than he had remembered her, James had not even noticed the difference in her dress.

Ariel looked down at her plate, stifling a smile. The young girl was quite besotted. They were certain to grow out of it before long. Clare was younger in spirit than her sixteen years and this was her first taste of admiration. Ariel herself had never been besieged by admirers, but at least Henry had braved Uncle Sylvester's disapproval to call upon her, and no one had called upon Clarissa. She would forget James quickly enough when the beaux of London crowded about her as her cousin was certain they would soon be doing.

Both of the girls were overwhelmed when they saw the size of the house which he intended to show them, for several houses the size of Sylvester's could have been placed within it with space to spare. It was built of weathered gray stone, four storys high, and more than a dozen gleaming windows looked out upon the square.

"Oh, how can we ever care for such a place?" Clarissa gasped, startled out of her customary meekness by the enormity of the task.

"There is no need to concern yourself about that, if this is the place you wish," Mr. MacPherson told her, completely ignoring Ariel, who had barely prevented herself from gaping at the magnificence of the building. Even her imagination, much more lively than her cousin's, had never envisioned anything like this.

"The place is completely staffed," James was saying, "and the servants so well trained that you will have to do no more than to state your wishes. Come, let me show you."

When he had introduced the butler, Hodges, who in turn presented the house-keeper, his wife, both Ariel and Clarissa felt at once that nothing would be beyond the capabilities of this couple. Hodges greeted them with a surface deference beneath which they sensed the pomposity of a most superior servant, making both girls wonder if they could ever accustom themselves to giving orders to someone so grand. His wife, as thin as her husband was fat, appeared to be a creature of boundless energy.

As she showed them about the house, trailed for much of the time by James MacPherson who was determined not to allow the younger lady out of his sight longer than need be, the girls were to find that, although they could not think the housekeeper would ever be described as the motherly type, she was far from being the nose-in-the-air type that her husband appeared to be.

Yet, beneath both Hodges' ponderous dignity and Mrs. Hodges' obvious competence, the young ladies received the feeling that they were being welcomed to the house. They could not guess how much of this sudden welcome was due to the fact that none of the servants had received their wage in some weeks.

When it had been arranged that the house would be put up for hire, Sir Percy Rawls had hoped to have the servants' salaries included in the money which was to be paid to him, But MacPherson and Son had dealt with him quite firmly upon that score. Everyone in the firm was aware that any money sent to him would end in some gamester's pocket or some ladybird's fist, while the servants remained unpaid.

He would, they had told him, receive a small portion of the hire of the house for his use, the greater part of it going to his creditors, and the new tenants would be responsible for paying the servants. Feeling much put upon, Sir Percy had protested profanely and at great length, but had at last agreed, since only the intervention of the firm into his affairs and its promise that his creditors would be paid in time had kept him out of the Fleet.

The interior of the house was found to be more impressive than the exterior, for Mrs. Hodges had seen to the removal of the Holland covers from all the furniture as soon as she had been given the word that two ladies – two *wealthy* ladies – were desirous of viewing the house. She had also harried the other servants for most of the night, until every surface, from floors to chandeliers, was cleaned and polished.

From the front hall with its marble floor and grand staircase, the young ladies had followed her about listening to her descriptions of the treasures to be seen. They might be ignorant of the comparative values of Meissen and Sevres, but, having done their own housework for years, they could appreciate the great amount of work which had gone into the preparing of this place for their inspection. Not even a speck of dust had been allowed to remain in the intricate carvings which could be seen wherever they looked.

Guided by Mrs. Hodges, they visited so many bedrooms that they had lost count of the number – being invited in each one to test the softness of the bed and having their attention called to the richness of the hangings – had exclaimed over the several drawing rooms and the huge library, admired both the large and small dining rooms, and had stood in awe in the center of the magnificent ballroom with its mirrored walls. Now they beamed upon Mrs. Hodges as Ariel exclaimed,

"Oh yes, this is exactly what we wish."

Mrs. Hodges curtsied, restraining an

impulse to beam back at them, for, aside from the pleasant prospect of being paid, she found both the young ladies to be most agreeable and thought they would prove to be excellent mistresses, willing to leave the entire running of the house to her, as they ought to do. "I am happy that your ladyship is pleased," she said sincerely.

"Your ladyship." No one had ever called her that except for the landlord at the posting inn and the red-haired guest who had prompted him to do so, even though *he* had not believed her. Ariel had always been aware that she possessed the title, but Sylvester, fearing that it might prove an incentive to extravagance upon her part, although he could not have explained how she could be extravagant when he gave her no money, had forbidden her to use it, telling her it would make her appear too high in the instep and would displease the neighbors.

Hearing herself so addressed brought a new thought. In the midst of such grandeur as this, she and Clare could scarcely wait upon themselves or help each other dress, as they had been in the habit of doing. Also, having ordered so many new gowns and other items of clothing, they would need someone to keep them in order. She, at least, had no intention of spending all her time at such tasks.

"Mrs. Hodges, my cousin and I did not bring any servants from the country." There was no need for anyone to be told that there had not been any servants to bring; let it seem that they had not wished to be transplanted to the city, as might well happen. "Is there someone among your staff who might serve as a lady's maid? Of course, we shall each have one, but we might manage with one between us for several days, until we have time to look about and engage someone for each of us."

Mrs. Hodges half closed her eyes, as if reviewing the servants under her command. "The thing is, my lady, that the Dowager took her dresser with her when she went to the country, and as Sir Percy, the present baronet, is a bachelor, there has been no need for lady's maids in the house of late."

Ariel grimaced, for she had not the least idea of how she should go about finding servants and had not thought about having to do so until now. She had never employed any and thought it must be especially difficult in a large place like London.

The housekeeper, however, had been giving more thought to the members of her staff and said, "I do believe that Nancy has had some experience along that line in her last position. It might be that she could be of some help until you have found the one you wish. It would only need to be for a short time. With your ladyship's permission, Mr. Hodges might contact the domestic agency and interview some young persons, having any he thinks satisfactory present themselves for your approval, of course."

Much impressed by the smooth manner in which Mrs. Hodges appeared to be able to handle every question which arose, Ariel said faintly that it would do nicely. She added that there had not yet been a discussion of price with Mr. MacPherson, but that both she and her cousin were so well pleased with the house that she had no doubt an agreement would be reached and that the ladies would wish to take possession as soon as they might be permitted to do so.

"If I may be permitted to say so, my lady," the redoubtable housekeeper said, "we shall be most happy to have you here. I shall give orders to have your bedchambers prepared at once, if you will state your preferences. Sir Percy, as you may have noticed, neglected to take a number of his belongings from his room. I have not had them packed away, but will do so if you would like that room, my lady."

Ariel recalled that, in showing the rooms, Mrs. Hodges had mentioned that one of them had been occupied by Sir Percy. If she recalled the right one, it had a very masculine – and, to her mind, somewhat forbidding – appearance, so she said hastily, "No, I think not. There is no reason not to leave the things where they are unless Sir Percy decides to send for them. There are so many other rooms, all of them beautiful, I am certain we shall have no trouble in finding ones to please us. Which one would you like to have, Clare?"

"If you do not wish it yourself," her cousin said with her usual hesitant manner, "I thought that the blue one was very nice."

"I wish you will stop behaving as if you were a charity child," Ariel said sharply. Then, seeing the hurt look which came into Clarissa's eyes, she went on, "I am sorry, dear. I do not wish to be cross with you, but you know we have always shared whatever we have and we shall continue to do so. However, you *must* learn to assert yourself. Now, say it quite firmly – 'I wish the blue room.' "

"I wish the blue room," Clarissa said obediently, but without a hint of firmness in her voice.

"See, you can do it if you try." Ariel hugged her and Mrs. Hodges smiled upon them both, thinking that she and Hodges could consider themselves fortunate in their new mistresses.

After his mother had retired to the country, Sir Percy had frequently filled the house with his drinking and gambling companions. They roistered about, caring nothing for the damage they might inflict upon the heirloom furniture or how many pieces of the best china they might smash. They frightened the younger maids with their improper attentions and flaunted their low bred women.

The servants could only be happy when the baronet was forced to leave London and Mrs. Hodges thought how pleasant and peaceful it would be to have a pair of nice young ladies in the house instead, although she privately thought that, despite her rank, the older one was apt to turn out to be something of a madcap.

None of this was evident in her voice as she said, "The blue room? Certainly. And which would you like, my lady?"

"There are so many." Ariel could scarcely remember which of them was which. Then she recalled Madame Josette's advice about choosing vivid colors and said, "There was a gold room. Yes, that is the one I wish. Each of them has a dressing room, and I shall be just across the hall from you, Clare, so that we can gossip at bedtime."

Entirely satisfied with everything they had seen about the house and assured by Mrs.

75

Hodges that they had overlooked nothing except the servants' quarters, which she did not think would interest them, the young ladies went along the hall to rejoin Mr. MacPherson, who had remained behind when they had gone to inspect the bedrooms. He would have liked very much to see the place where the lady of his heart would spend her nights, but considered it would be extremely improper for him to do so.

They chattered happily over everything they had seen. It was difficult to tell whether they were more impressed with the carved mantel in the front drawing room, which, although they did not know it and would not have recognized the name, had been designed by the great Robert Adam, or by the closed stove in the kitchen. Perhaps the latter, for, with no intention of using it themselves, they could appreciate its convenience.

Listening to them, James began to glow with self-pride. His father would certainly approve of the manner in which he had contrived to serve several clients at one time, assisting Lady Ariel in getting settled in London and, in doing so, solving at least a part of Sir Percy's indebtedness.

"When may we take possession?" Ariel asked him eagerly when they had finally thought of nothing more to praise.

"As soon as you like. Since our firm is handling the house as well as your accounts, there will be no need for delays. If you wish to stay at this moment, I can bring over the necessary papers." That would be an excuse for another call upon the ladies and he felt that he had been quite clever to think of it.

Ariel was about to agree with him but, after a moment's thought and a wordless communication with her cousin, said, "No, I think that, if you do not mind escorting us there, we should go to your office and sign them. That will allow Mrs. Hodges time enough to prepare for us. Also, we must go to Grillon's to pay our account, if you should have the time to take us, and to collect our things. Oh, and there are the shops that we visited yesterday. We cannot take your time for that, but we must go and tell them where our purchases are to be sent."

"Your ladyship need not put yourself to such trouble," Mrs. Hodges told her just as James was about to declare his willingness to take them anywhere. "If you will give me a list of the shops, a footman can be sent to collect any parcels which are ready and leave orders to have the others sent here."

"Th-thank you, Mrs. Hodges," Ariel said, overwhelmed by so much service. "I shall make up such a list when I return."

Some moments later in James MacPherson's carriage with the young man seated between them – not quite certain in his mind how he had been fortunate enough to have been placed beside his angel, but thinking that, but for Mrs. Hodges, he would have been able to accompany her for several more hours – Ariel began to laugh softly.

" 'Your ladyship need not concern herself!' Oh, this is beyond anything wonderful. After all these years of doing without things which we ought to have had, now to have this magnificent house, footmen to run errands for us, and no one to tell us we cannot spend as much as we wish. Oh, Clare, are you not happy to be here?"

On the verge of making a fervent agreement, Clarissa turned to see James' admiring gaze upon her and completely forgot what she had been about to say. She looked away quickly, wishing again that she could refrain from blushing at his obvious regard, quite unaware of the hopes aroused in the young gentleman at the sight of that rosy glow.

FIVE

It might be thought that one who was totally unaccustomed to living in luxury might find some trouble in adjusting to such a different mode of life, but neither of the young ladies experienced the slightest difficulty in doing so. It was most agreeable to have everything done for them, from having their morning chocolate fetched to their bedrooms to having parcels fetched and messages delivered, to carrying upstairs the water for their baths – baths scented with jasmine, lilac, or more exotic scents, which need not be hurried and from which they arose to be tenderly enveloped in large, soft towels.

Even the simple task of buttoning each other's gowns, which they had done since they were in pinafores, was now done for them. As Mrs. Hodges had promised, her husband had quickly found several "young persons" for Lady Ariel to interview as possible lady's maids. The first of these was a gaunt individual who had once been dresser for a duchess, whose name she took pains to mention a number of times while being interviewed by her ladyship.

It was obvious from her conversation about Her Grace and from the airs she gave herself that she could have considered it quite a comedown for one of her consequence to serve the mere daughter of an earl, and Ariel was certain that she would never be comfortable in the presence of so superior a servant, so chose instead a younger female of lesser experience but greater amiability, who answered to the name of Parsons.

She admitted with some reluctance that her given name was Molly, but Ariel gathered the impression that, among the members of the *ton*, it was not customary to call servants by their first names, unless perhaps in the case of very minor members of the staff. She did feel, however, that she could be comfortable with Parsons as soon as she was able to remember that she was not to do the slightest thing for herself, even to fastening her cuffs or tying her garters.

The question of an abigail for Clarissa had been quickly solved, for that young lady declared, with a firmness which surprised and delighted her cousin, that if she could not have Nancy she would have no servant at all.

"I like her," Clarissa insisted, "and I think she likes me, too, although I am certain she is too well trained to say so. I could not be happy with some of the young women you have seen. They frighten me."

"I know how you feel," Ariel admitted, laughing. "The Duchess' dresser, for example; she frightened me. However, Parsons will do me very well."

"And Nancy will do for me. It may not be the fashion, but I am going to call her Nancy; she does not mind – I think she prefers it. Her surname is Frowse. Imagine calling her *that!* I know I should feel as if I was calling a dog every time I spoke to her."

"Of course you may call her whatever you wish," Ariel assured her, thinking that the visit to London was going to be a good thing for Clare. Already, she was beginning to assert herself in a manner she had never dared to do at home.

Ariel had provided Mrs. Hodges with the promised list of shops, warning her that there would be a great many items to be collected. Two footmen had been dispatched and had returned laden with parcels which Parsons received with outward indifference and inward curiosity, while Nancy was openly excited about all the beautiful clothing which she would be handling for her mistress.

Much to the surprise of the young ladies, Madame Josette had sent along several gowns which had been completed for each of them.

They were delighted to receive these, for each had only the single gown from their first visit to the shop and, although they had been accustomed at home to wearing the same gown day after day, they knew already that it was not the accepted thing in the city.

Madame Josette had long ago reached the position where it was no longer necessary for her to put the members of her establishment to any trouble to please a client if she did not wish to do so. Any lady of the *ton* would wait as long as required for the privilege of being seen in a gown whose cut labeled it at once as a Josette creation and clients were aware that they must bespeak gowns well in advance of important occasions if they were to be certain of receiving them at the proper time.

It was an unfortunate thing, Josette considered, that so many of those who could afford her gowns did not display them to the best advantage. One Duke's daughter was so rail-thin that no amount of discreet tucks or puffs could make her appear to have a figure, and if she appeared in one of the sheer gowns so beloved by certain of the great ladies, the result was appalling.

Another's teeth protruded to such an extent that one was more apt to be conscious of them than of the gown she wore, and there were several like the Honourable Myrtle Soames, whose fondness for sweets resulted both in the unsightly bulges which spoiled the fit of any gown and in her already sallow complexion throwing out spots, usually at the very time she had been invited to some grand function.

There were also the former beauties, well past their prime, who insisted upon wearing gowns which would be more suitable for their daughters – or granddaughters – and dowagers whose sagging flesh was mercilessly exposed by the décolletage they preferred.

There were, of course, those whose faces and figures were all that a designer could ask, but many of these were derelict in the payment of their accounts, uncaring that even a couturiere must eat and pay her employees. It was rarely that Madame was fortunate enough to obtain a client of such fortune as Lady Ariel could boast, if she wished to do so, who also possessed a form which could display to advantage either the most regal or the most dashing of her fashions. Also, her petite cousin was the perfect model for the loveliest *jeune fille* styles.

A designer could not ask for a more satisfactory pair and, having assured herself that all their bills would be paid promptly, Madame was determined that no other than herself should touch them. They must be seen only in gowns recognizable as having come from the hands of Josette. Therefore she ordered her seamstresses to put aside the work they were doing for all her other clients until a respectable wardrobe had been completed for Lady Ariel and Miss Morwin.

As Madame had predicted, word of the arrival in the city of two very wealthy beauties had quickly circulated throughout the *ton*. An eyebrow was raised here and there when it was learned they were unchaperoned but, since her ladyship was a widow, it was only the highest sticklers who dared to asperse their conduct.

Almost at once, cards were being left at the house in Cavendish Square and a respectable number of invitations came after them – so many, in fact, that it would have been quite impossible for the ladies to accept them all.

"Now, how shall we know which of these we ought to attend and which we may omit?" Ariel asked, sorting through the cards engraved with names she did not recognize. "I did not expect that there would be so many, at least not so soon. There is no way that we can know which of these are important people – the ones we ought not to insult. We shall just have to have Hodges find a secretary who can tell us about such things."

"Until we are able to secure one," Clarissa said diffidently, "perhaps Ja – Mr.

MacPherson – might be able to advise us."

"I wonder –" Ariel pondered the question for some moments, while her cousin watched her hopefully. It had been several days since they had seen the young man, for he had been able to think of no further reason for calling. Although she would never be so bold as to suggest that they should visit his office, their need of assistance might serve as a reason for seeking him out.

"At least, it will do no harm to speak to him about it," the older girl said at last. "If he cannot help us, he might know of someone who can do so."

Accordingly, a note was dispatched to MacPherson and Son, saying that the ladies would be thankful for some advice from Mr. MacPherson, if he would not find it inconvenient to call upon them.

Upon his return to the city, the elder Mr. MacPherson had been full of praise, a commodity which he normally dealt out only sparingly, for his son because of the manner in which James had solved the problems of Lady Ariel and Sir Percy at the same time.

Under the management of the firm, Lady Ariel's fortune, which had not been an insignificant one at the time of Lord Watling's death, had been increased during her minority until she was one of their wealthiest clients.

When her ladyship's message arrived, it was naturally given into the hands of the head of the firm, who read it carefully, then passed it to James.

"I should like to see my old friend's daughter, but that must wait, for I have some things urgently requiring my attention. Lady Ariel seems to be pleased with the manner in which you have been serving her, so I think it might be a good thing if you were to hold yourself available to assist her whenever she wishes" – a command which his son received with such enthusiasm as to make his father wonder, for it was unlike the "boy" to take such an interest in their clients.

Despite the fact that he was not himself a member of the *ton*, James MacPherson was well enough informed, through the dealings of his own firm and through acquaintances in other companies, to give the ladies the advice they sought; at the same time telling them that, unless Lady Ariel found herself in need of a secretary for other purposes, they might call upon him at any time for aid.

A number of the invitations were pronounced to be unexceptionable and James encouraged them to send acceptances; several others, he tossed to one side, labeling the writers as mushrooms and unworthy even of an answer.

"What of this one?" Ariel asked, showing him a message which had just been received from a Mrs. Mossmin, who expressed herself delighted by the arrival in London of the daughter of her lamented but very dear friend. She hoped that "dear little Ariel" would allow her to take the place of her Mama in presenting her to the *ton*.

"I do not remember anyone of that name, but I was very young and, of course, Uncle Sylvester did not correspond with any of my parents' friends. He would have thought it an unnecessary expense."

James shook his head decidedly.

"A nobody," he declared. "I would doubt that she ever saw your parents or would be able to tell you their names, since you are pretending that Laurence was your husband's name – which, if you will permit me to say so, I do not think you should do. Certainly, it is unlikely that she was ever their friend. You will notice that she makes no explanation of the occasion of the friendship."

"You are right; she does not. I ought to have thought of that, ought I not? Surely, if she had gone to school with my Mama or had attended her wedding, or anything of the kind, she would have said so."

"At the risk of sounding a gossip, I must tell you that it is said that Mrs. Mossmin has but to brush shoulders with someone of importance at Hookham's Library or buy a ribbon on the same day in the Pantheon Bazaar, and immediately she begins referring to her 'dear friend, Lady So-and-So.' She toad-eats everyone of importance. As for her offer to present you to the *ton*, she could not do so, but only wishes to hang onto your skirts and meet *your* important friends."

"How horrible it would have been for us if we had called upon her, which we might have done had we not had you to warn us," Clarissa exclaimed, then collapsed into blushing confusion at the thought of having been so forward.

James was almost equally overcome by such praise from his adored one and Ariel glanced from one to the other, struggling to hide her amusement. She was grateful to the young man for his help and, indeed, they would not have known how to get on without his aid at this time, but now she wondered if it would have been better to have made other arrangements, so that her cousin would see less of him.

Still, the attraction was harmless enough and it would be only a short time until Clarissa would have hordes of important admirers. Then Mr. MacPherson would be retired to his proper place in her life – or rather, out of it.

After a moment, she was able to speak of the other invitations which she had received with praiseworthy gravity. When all of these matters had been settled, the young man asked if he could be of help to them in any other way and thinking that, since he was already here, she might as well make use of his services, Ariel asked, "How ought we to go about obtaining some horses, sir? I have noticed that there are several carriages in the carriage house and the stables are large, but empty."

A bit guiltily, she thought for the first time in several days of the young horse she had purchased on her way to London, which was still stabled near Grillon's Hotel. She would give orders to have it brought around, but it would not be enough for them.

She had never seen a carriage drawn by a single horse, in fact she doubted that a single horse could do so, and she refused to be seen abroad in the old gig. To her mind, the vehicle screamed of the poverty they had left behind them.

"I should have seen to that matter for you some time ago," Mr. MacPherson said in some embarrassment. "The stables used to be well stocked, but Sir Percy took away as many of his horses as he could manage before his creditors seized the others. But how have you been getting about without a rig?"

"We have taken a hackney, very much to Hodges' disapproval each time that he must order one for us."

"I do not wonder at that, since he was accustomed to Sir Percy's large stables." The young man was also shocked at the idea of his angel having to ride in a common hackney, and her ladyship as well, of course. "But I am surprised that he did not inform you that there was no need –" He rose and went to the bell pull, saying as he grasped it, "With your permission, Lady Ariel?"

She nodded, wondering as to his purpose. When Hodges appeared, puffing slightly from having hurried, Mr. MacPherson asked, "Is not Fraser about, Hodges?"

"He is, presently, sir, having returned only last evening from a long visit to his parents, not having any thought that he would be needed, you understand, sir." In Hodges' tone, there was a slight indication that the upper orders had been at fault for not having made the matter entirely clear to the servants.

James nodded. "With both Sir Percy and the horses gone, of course; however, there will be work for him in the future. Will you have him fetched, please?"

When Hodges withdrew to send a summons to the other man, pleased with having made it plain that Fraser was not to be held to blame in any manner for his defection, the young man said, "Fraser is – was – Sir Percy's head coachman. I doubt if you will find a better judge of horseflesh in all of London. I am surprised, however, that he has not permitted himself to be lured away into some other household since Sir Percy – departed. I have heard it said that even Lord Dexter offered him a position. Since his lordship has been out of the city for some weeks, it may be that Fraser has only been waiting for his return to make the change."

"Lord Dexter?" The name had a familiar sound, although Ariel could not recall having seen it among the many invitations. Still, if the gentleman was out of the city, she could scarcely have received anything from him. Clarissa also tried to recall where they had heard it, tugging at a curl as if to stir her memory in that fashion.

"Randall Vernon, the Right Honourable, the Earl of Dexter." The manner in which young James pronounced the name and the full title caused Ariel to say,

"You do not care for Lord Dexter, Mr. MacPherson?"

"I have no right to say anything of him, since I know him only by reputation. Naturally, I do not move in the same circles as he. He is known as the *nonpareil*. Reputed to have excellent taste in horses and –" He broke off, coloring.

"And in women, I think you were about to say?" Ariel asked, amused at what appeared to her to be a slight priggishness in the young man's manner. It might be entertaining to shock him a bit. "Do you mean that he is a rake? How interesting; I have heard of them, but have never met one."

James frowned, thinking that a lady ought not to admit even to a knowledge of such things, and Clarissa touched her cousin's arm, saying, "The man we saw at the posting inn. Did he not say that his name was Dexter?"

"The red-haired man?" Ariel flushed at the remembrance of the lazy voice calling her a pretty piece. Within the short time since her arrival, she had acquired enough city knowledge to understand that he had *not* been complimenting her. "I believe that he did say something of the sort, and the landlord called him 'Your Lordship.' A most arrogant person; I trust we shall not meet *him* again."

"I fear that you will do so, if that was Lord Dexter, and I presume that it may have been from your description. He is certainly both red-haired and arrogant. He is received in all the best circles, despite his reputation.

Hostesses are willing to overlook much when a gentleman has both wealth and title. But I trust that your ladyship will have nothing to do with him if you should happen to meet."

"It is most unlikely." Ariel dismissed Lord Dexter with a shrug as Hodges returned, announcing, "Fraser is here, my lady."

The coachman was a small, wiry man, appearing even less impressive beside the butler's portly form. He scarcely looked as if he would be able to handle a pair, much less a spirited team, and Ariel considered him with some doubt.

Mr. MacPherson, however, assured her that she could depend upon Fraser in every way and, when told that her ladyship wished to procure horses, the coachman promised volubly to find her the best available in London or outside of it, should there not be suitable cattle to be found at present within the city.

"Just how many would you be wantin', my lady?"

"For the present, a team only – but it must be an outstanding one, a team which will cause everyone to take notice of it. We shall want more later, at least several riding horses. After that, we shall see. And what of a carriage? Shall I need to buy one?"

"That depends on what sort of rig you

want, my lady. There's one in the carriage house now, but it belonged to Lady Rawls, Sir Percy's mother. She has been livin' with her married daughter in Yorkshire these past two years and there's no need for it there. 'Tis well built enough, I'll admit, but not in the latest fashion; 'twas not, even when her ladyship was a usin' of it.''

"If that is so, it certainly will not do for us; we must have the latest mode. You must find us one, Fraser. The horses, too, as I said, must be of the finest, regardless of cost. We must have them for Lady Mayne's tea, day after tomorrow. It will not be at all the thing for us to make our first appearance in society in a hackney.''

She had not expected that they would not do so, but that was before she had learned about Fraser. Now the idea was *unthinkable*. She *must* have her own carriage, and at once.

"Mr. MacPherson will see to the expense, will you not?''

That gentleman agreed at once and Fraser looked at him skeptically, thinking that he scarcely looked the kind to be gifting his favorites with expensive bits of blood. The coachman showed more respect when he learned that Mr. MacPherson was a member of the firm which handled her ladyship's affairs.

To have one's man of business so agreeable to sporting any amount of blunt bespoke a great deal of it to be had and Fraser was no different from any of the other servants in wishing to be paid. Too often, the money that should have come to them had found its way to some Captain Sharp instead. He agreed that the carriage and the "prads" would be at her ladyship's service on the morrow and withdrew to begin at once to negotiate for an outfit he knew of.

Clarissa took this opportunity to inquire shyly of James if he would be attending Lady Mayne's tea and was greatly disappointed when he said that he would not.

"It would be so much nicer if there would be someone there whom we knew; the thought of facing so many strangers frightens me." She had forgotten that, only days ago, he had also been a stranger.

"You need not worry," he assured her. "They will all be your friends at once."

"It will not be the same," she protested, then wondered if he would think that she had been too bold in expressing a preference for his society.

James, however, declared that he was honored that she should think of him as a friend and was about to add that he would serve her in any possible way with the greatest of pleasure when Ariel, having dismissed Hodges after requesting him to order a hackney for what both of them hoped would be the last time, turned to say:

"I regret that we shall not have time to talk with you any longer just at present, Mr. MacPherson. It seems unkind to send you away so abruptly after all the kindness you have shown us today. Indeed, I do not know what we should have done if you had not come to our aid. However, we have a number of errands. And Madame Josette has found a hairdresser who will call upon us this afternoon, so we must make haste now. We cannot keep him waiting."

"Indeed not," he said gallantly. "One might be forgiven for making a duchess wait, but never a hairdresser."

Ariel looked at him sharply, wondering if there had been irony in the remark, then deciding that there had not been. "So I have been given to understand. And again, let me thank you for all of the help you have given us."

"You may call upon me at any time," the young man assured her, but it was at Clarissa he looked as he spoke.

SIX

Both Ariel and Clarissa felt that the conference with James MacPherson had been a rewarding one, for they had learned a great deal about the people they might meet in the days to come. However, that talk, plus the discussion with Fraser about obtaining the necessary conveyance – which had also been most satisfactory – had taken more time than they had planned, so that they were forced to put off a part of their shopping until the morrow.

Madame Josette had warned them that it would never do for them to keep this particular hairdresser waiting; he could have his share of important clients and it was only upon a recommendation from her (she omitted to mention the hint she had given him about her ladyship's openhandedness) that he had been persuaded to add their names to his list.

Born in Shoreditch and having been informed by his mother that, to the best of her knowledge, his father had been a gentleman by the name of Lamb, young Tony had discovered that, instead of the usual pursuits favored by his companions, he had a talent for the cutting and arranging of ladies' hair which amounted almost to genius. Ignoring the scornful comments of the others, he followed this line of work but enjoyed only a mild success until told by Josette, who had known him when she was still Josie, that his English name would be against him if he aspired to be taken up by the *ton*.

With her help, he Gallicized it to Antoine Agneau and allowed hints to creep into his conversation to the effect that he was a refugee because so many of his French clients had been among the now-headless nobility. This was enough to cause him to be taken up immediately by the English ladies who felt that in a way they were striking a blow against the now-defeated Bonaparte by employing this young man. No better at comparing dates than he, none of them realized that he was much too young to have served the Old Regime, and most of them soon vowed that they would have no one except Monsieur Antoine to touch their hair.

Entering the room and placing his implements upon the table, he then spent several minutes in observing the two young ladies critically and, having learned early in his career that rudeness only endeared him to his clients who were so high in the instep that others were forever toad-eating them, informed them that they resembled a pair of milkmaids rather than ladies of the *ton*, adding, "But that is why you need Antoine, of course. Who else could give you the touch you need?"

Having been informed by Josette that it was Lady Ariel who would be paying his bill, he approached her first. Catching her chin, he turned her head this way and that, studying the lines of her nose and chin, the curve of her dark brows and, brushing back her hair, examining the shape of her ears and noting the manner in which her hair grew down to a peak in the middle of her forehead.

It was difficult for Ariel not to draw back from his touch, but she was able to convince herself that, after all, he was merely a hairdresser and she must not think of him as a man. This decision on her part would have come as a great surprise to Antoine, who, despite having the appearance of an exquisite, actually enjoyed quite a reputation as a gallant among the ladies of his acquaintance.

"Your ladyship would be well advised to adopt a daring mode," he said at last, having been prompted by Josette as to the lady's tastes and happy to find that she agreed with his own opinion. He would have insisted that she accept his decision in any case, but it was much simpler when the lady did not argue.

"Oh yes, that is what I wish, very dashing," Ariel exclaimed, then held her breath as comb and scissors began flying and black curls fell about her recklessly.

She wanted to cry out to him to stop, then recalled that the new Ariel Laurence was to be as different as possible from the girl who had been held down all her life by Sylvester's clutch-penny ways. If she must sacrifice *all* of her hair to accomplish that purpose she would do so. She sat in silence, wondering if that would actually be her fate.

At last, when she felt that she must be completely shorn, comb and scissors were laid aside and Antoine placed a mirror in her hands, exclaiming, *"Voila!"* one of the few French words to which he had been able to adapt his English tongue.

Ariel stared into the glass, scarcely recognizing herself. The back of her hair had been cropped quite short; across her brow and before her ears, a few feathery curls lay in casual fashion, while the rest of her hair had been drawn up to lie in a mass of curls across the top of her head and down either side to half cover her ears. She had never imagined that she could look like this.

"Oh, I like it," she said softly.

"But of course," Antoine told her grandly.

No one had ever dared to criticize his handiwork.

He was aware that the comment would have been much more effective if he could have uttered it in French, but he was one of those individuals who had absolutely no ear for any foreign tongue and must content himself with adopting a faint accent which passed among his clients for French. The few occasions on which he had been rash enough to assay the language itself, it was to discover that many of the ladies he served were much more conversant with it than he. On one occasion it had cost him a client for, in attempting to tell her that she would strike her guests like a flame, his tongue had betrayed him into saying, *"flan,"* rather than, *"flamme."* Understandably, the lady objected to being told she would be thrown at the assemblage like a soft desert. From that moment, Antoine had not dared attempt any flights into French.

"It must always be done exactly so," he said sternly to Parsons, who, with Nancy, had been summoned to watch so that they could arrange their young ladies' hair when the master was not available.

Parsons grunted, giving the young exquisite a sour look. He might be able to fool the Quality with his dandified airs, she thought, but she was certain that she could have named his birthplace within a few streets, having come from the same area herself; but she had improved her station by proper English labor, not by aping foreign ways.

Antoine was aware that she suspected his origin, but doubted that he had any reason to fear her betrayal of him. It was not the habit of ladies to engage in gossip of that sort with their servants. In fact, had he realized it, Lady Ariel would not have minded in the least that he was not French, for it was his artistry which charmed her.

Now, turning to Clarissa, he said, "And a style for you, young miss." *Mademoiselle* was another of the words which had defeated him in the past and he feared to risk using it on this occasion.

The younger girl drew back, alarmed. "Oh no – what you have done for Ariel looks wonderfully, but I could not –"

"Oh, that is never for you," he said soothingly. "Come, let me show you what I have in mind for you. You need not fear."

Although nearly terrified by the thought that he might become carried away by an urge to do something unusual with her hair, Clarissa gave herself into his hands, wincing every time she heard the snick of the scissors.

However, they were used only rarely, to snip a few errant strands.

Most of his work was done with the comb, drawing her hair back into soft waves, then fastening it upon the nape of her neck so that a cluster of curls fell down her back in what was almost a schoolgirl style, with only one large golden curl brought forward to lie upon her left shoulder.

The arrangement was one which would have been excellent upon a china shepherdess; it was perfect for Clarissa, who exclaimed over it in the same awed tones that Ariel had used for her style. Nancy, too, received Antoine's instructions as to her mistress' coiffure and promised to follow them faithfully, happy that the arrangement was one well within her abilities to achieve.

Pocketing a fee which was so large that he would have feared to ask for it if Josette had not encouraged him to do so, Antoine bowed himself out, promising that he would be at the ladies' call whenever they wished him; like Josette, he was plagued by many clients who were slow to pay and found Ariel's openhandedness much to his liking. The girls were left to rhapsodize about each other's coiffures and to wonder if it would be necessary for them to shop upon the morrow, or if they might attend Lady Mayne's tea

103

in some of the new gowns they already possessed.

"Did you ever dream, Clare," Ariel asked, "that we could possibly have so many gowns that we must wonder which of them we ought to wear?" and her cousin blissfully agreed that she had never done so.

Fraser had proven as good as his word, having discovered a team of perfectly matched blacks, each of them without a single white hair. The carriage which was offered with them was something out of the common way, but Fraser, having privately decided that his new mistress was one who was wishful of cutting a dash, thought she would like it.

It had been constructed to the order of a nabob and was as black as the cattle, except for its lavish trimming of gold – which had been repeated in the decorations upon the harness – but it was its upholstery which set it apart from others of its kind.

During the time he had spent in India, the nabob had been able to perform some service, which in his opinion had been trifling, for a maharajah and had in return been gifted with the pelts of several snow leopards. Upon his return to England he had decided, rather than hanging the skins upon the walls or using them as rugs, to have his carriage upholstered with them, the whole to be a gift to his new wife.

The lady was entranced with the horses and with the appearance of the carriage, but, having taken a dislike to the fur, declared that it made her sneeze and demanded that her husband have it replaced with more conventional material. A crimson velvet would have been her choice. The gentleman, however, was piqued by what he considered her lack of appreciation for his gift and declared that if she would not have the fur, she would have nothing, not even the cattle which she begged him to keep, and offered the entire outfit for sale. The price was so extreme that not everyone could afford it, but Lady Ariel could do so. Fraser had no trouble in securing it, provided she approved.

"I don't know as you'll care for it, m'lady, it bein' a bit out of the usual," he declared when displaying it to her, although he was almost certain what her answer would be.

As he had expected, Ariel was entranced.

"No one in London will have anything to compare with it," she cried and ordered that the bill should be sent along to MacPherson and Son for payment.

The elder Mr. MacPherson, a thrifty but not miserly man, was beginning to exclaim over the great number of charges which were put against Lady Ariel's account, but when his son told him of the early life of his ladyship, he shook his head with a dour smile.

"I suppose it is not surprising, then, that she wishes to spend so much. Fortunately, she does not appear to care for gaming, nor have her expenditures for jewelery been great, so there is no doubt her account can withstand the charges. We must hope that she soon has all the fripperies she wishes."

Ariel's only regret in purchasing the carriage was that she could not have the Laurence arms emblazoned upon its doors. Since she was supposed to be a widow, however, her lozenge would have had to include her "husband's" arms as well as her own, and she did not dare to fabricate them. Too many people would have recognized at once that no such arms existed. She might have pretended that the Laurence arms had been her husband's and that she had none of her own but, for some reason, she shrank from doing so and was forced to content herself with having an unmatched vehicle and team.

Lady Mayne was elated that hers was the first invitation that the very wealthy young ladies had accepted and lost no time in spreading the word that they might be met at her house that afternoon. The result was that many of her guests found that they would be accompanied by sons or brothers who had hitherto refused to attend such affairs, labeling them much too dull for their liking.

"They're rumored to be beauties, of course," one commented wryly, "but no doubt they'll turn out to be a pair of homely Joans like most of the heiresses we know."

"That is true – sad to say," his friend replied, "but they also say that the widow is completely the mistress of her own fortune and that it is a large one, so I think she may be forgiven if she turns out to be a bit butter-toothed."

"Yes, it is wonderful how much a coating of gold can improve even the worst female," agreed the first.

So it was that Lady Mayne's rooms were filled almost to bursting when Ariel and Clarissa arrived and were greeted with enthusiasm by their hostess. This being their first appearance in public, they had taken great pains with their preparation. Ariel, after changing her mind several times, had finally decided upon a gown of violet, not the pale shade which was considered proper for half-mourning, but a deep violet gown of simple cut, made of a shimmering cloth so woven that its colors seemed to change whenever she moved.

Clarissa's gown was of the palest pink over

white satin, its skirt and sleeves a myriad of tiny ruffles, which caused one overimaginative young gentleman to liken her to a bonbon, much to his friends' amusement; privately several of them wished that they had thought of the description first. The contrast between the pair was remarkable, yet it would have been difficult to say which was the more attractive.

Lady Mayne drew them about the room, presenting them to so great a number of dowagers that they despaired of remembering the names of half of them. They were greeted gushingly or distantly by many young ladies, depending upon whether they were considered as future friends or rivals, and ogled by dozens of young gentlemen who were happy to learn that it was possible for a female to have both wealth and beauty – and, to complete the attraction, she had neither a strict father nor a guardian.

"Was it not wonderful?" Ariel demanded when at last they had been escorted to their carriage by a number of young Corinthians, who admired the perfection of their team, wondering where Fraser had found such prime bits of blood and bone.

The carriage and its exotic upholstery were also worthy of many envious comments and more than one dandy was determined that he would have something even more spectacular, although he might presently be at a loss to decide what it might be. It was certain that, in addition to the beauty of the ladies, the fame of Lady Ariel's carriage and four would be the talk of male London, just as their gowns had impressed the ladies.

"And only think," her ladyship went on happily, "of all the new invitations we have received from people we met today. We cannot possibly accept the half of them. Oh, we are going to enjoy every moment of our stay in London, are we not?"

"Y-yes." Despite the fact that she could not believe that any gathering which excluded young Mr. MacPherson from its lists could be considered perfect, still Clarissa could scarcely fail to be impressed by the weight of masculine admiration which had been her portion this afternoon. "Yes," she replied more firmly, "we are."

Lady Mayne's tea was only the first of the entertainments which the young ladies enjoyed; entertainments which piled upon one another so quickly that it seemed they would scarcely be able to find time for sleeping or for the shopping that these events required. They attended rout-parties and balls and soon learned that they must not confuse the two, although there was dancing at both.

Venetian breakfasts made them laugh when they were alone at the idea of a "breakfast" which began in midafternoon and lasted until all hours, and they wondered what these people would do if forced to arise before five in the morning to breakfast at that hour.

"Most of them have not even reached their beds by that hour," Ariel laughed.

"And it seems that we will soon be doing the same," her cousin agreed, thinking that there was sometimes too much excitement in their lives, although she had no desire to return to the sort of life they had lived in the country.

Dozens of beaux were eager to escort them to Ranelagh and to Vauxhall, where the fireworks displays were much admired and the famous ham duly praised, even though the country-bred girls wished that it had not been sliced *quite* so thin, as they were accustomed to more substance in their food.

A number of efforts were made to take strolls *a deux* along some of the secluded pathways and Ariel was sometimes tempted to consent, certain that she could discourage any improper advances on the part of her escort. Clarissa, however, would neither agree to go, nor consent to be left alone with some gentleman in their box The ladies remained in each other's company at all times and their beaux were reduced to the mildest of flirtations.

A journey to Richmond Park included an al fresco nuncheon, fortunately not disturbed by a shower, and, when Fraser had found them mounts of a dashing appearance but manageable disposition, there were rides in the Park in the midst of a group of admiring gentlemen, with frequent stops to visit with the occupants of the carriages which thronged its drives at the popular hour.

Madame Josette had designed their riding habits deliberately to invite comments. Ignoring the velvets, serges, and other heavy materials favored by her competitors, she had made up both outfits in twilled sarsenet, which was usually used for finer gowns. Ariel's was of vivid green, its masculine collar and stock belied by the manner in which the soft material was molded to her figure from shoulder to waist, then flaring as necessary to enable her to sit her horse, and with the skirt caught up at the side to display her embroidered boots.

Clarissa's habit was also in green, but in a delicate shade, and made with frill upon frill of the finest lace replacing the stock which Ariel wore. The older girl flaunted a tall shako of sable, while for Clarissa, Madame had decreed that the customary stiff hat be

111

discarded for a softer model draped with yards of veiling, so that it fell about her shoulders like a cloud.

Had such *outré* fashions been attempted by anyone else, the result would have been laughed out of London, but the combination of Lady Ariel's wealth and Madame Josette's recognizable touch caused the sensation which Madame intended and so many jealous ladies were soon demanding similar habits that she was forced to employ two more seamstresses. Ariel reveled in the attention she drew and even Clarissa could not fail to be thrilled at some of the compliments she was receiving, although she quailed beneath the dagger-glances thrown their way by less favored young ladies and was embarrassed by the leers of some of the older dandies, who tried to strike up an acquaintance with them.

There was only one place in London whose doors remained firmly closed to them – that unimpressive appearing but, to the *ton*, vastly important establishment in King Street. Not even the soft-hearted Lady Sefton nor Lady Jersey, who was so careless of her own reputation, could have been persuaded to offer those precious vouchers to Almack's to a pair of young ladies who jaunted about London without a chaperon.

Not even the fact that the elder of the two

ladies was a widow and the possessor of both a title and a fortune was enough to make their behavior palatable to those strict guardians of the Marriage Mart, even though one or two of them might privately welcome the pair into their homes.

Mrs. Drummond Burrell, who disapproved of nearly all of the ladies of the *ton* only to a slightly greater degree than she did of her fellow Patronesses, cast her eyes upon Ariel and applied her favorite, if often misused, term of condemnation for many aspirants.

"Farouche! No one is to offer them vouchers," she ordered, a command which might well have been ignored had it not been for the fact that for once all the other Patronesses agreed with her decision, if not with her description of the lady in question.

In many cases, this exclusion from those almost hallowed portals would have been the signal for other hostesses to strike the ladies from their invitation lists, but there were few whose sense of propriety outweighed their respect for the size of Lady Ariel's fortune.

Especially, the mamas of marriageable, and frequently impecunious, sons were anxious to number her ladyship among their friends, and the mamas of hopeful girls had soon become aware that where the widow and her cousin would be, the beaux could also be found in plenty. Even some of them, however, began to have second thoughts about her desirability after the whispers began.

In return for the many kindnesses which had been shown to her and Clarissa, Lady Ariel had given a tea, fearful that she was not yet capable of handling the complexities of managing a grand ball. Many of those who attended had not been able to see the interior of the house since Lady Rawls had gone to live in Yorkshire and were wondering what changes the newcomer might have made.

Those who were expecting to see furniture with crocodile feet or sphinxes adorning the Adam mantelpiece were doomed to disappointment, for Lady Ariel's sole changes had been to replace some of the most sadly worn carpets and draperies with new ones of the same style as the others. She had, however, substituted crimson or green in some cases for the bilious yellow which appeared to have been Lady Rawls' favorite color, but this change was approved by all except one or two of her callers.

Among the callers were Lady Soames and her daughter, whom Ariel had felt unable to exclude, even though she had frequently been the victim of barbed remarks from the pair. While her ladyship was secretly deploring the fact that there were no modern touches that

114

she could deprecate, Myrtle had slipped away upstairs on the excuse of needing to pin up a slight rent in her gown.

The gown, which had been made by a lesser dressmaker since Madame Josette had refused to make her anything so unbecoming, was loaded with so many yards of floss that its original design could scarcely be seen and any number of rents could have gone undetected. The Honourable Myrtle thought it gave her an air of fashion, unaware that she actually resembled a giant shuttlecock.

The excuse of a torn gown was one she had used in many other homes to enable her to push her nose, frequently adorned with several unsightly spots, into other people's possessions. The repairs, being largely imaginary, were quickly completed and she began prowling about Ariel's bedroom, peering first into the armoire. The gowns hanging there were a riot of color and amid them was one of peacock blue which she had no difficulty in recognizing as the one she had desired from Madame Josette.

It angered her to see that this newcomer, whom she labeled as an upstart despite the fact that Ariel's title was better than her own, had purchased the gown she had wanted, but she was happy to see that it bore none of the myriad of trimmings on which she would have insisted. She had noted what she considered this lack of taste in her ladyship's gowns before this.

Myrtle would not have wished to own any of the gowns she saw, for all of them were much too plain for her taste, but she did wish that her mother would allow her to have so many.

"Though it is not her fault," she muttered. "She would buy them for me if Papa did not always make such a scene about the bills."

Slamming the door upon the gowns, she wandered about the room, opening drawers and fingering toilet articles, making a note of the scarcity of paints upon Ariel's dressing table. *She* had far more at home. Going through the dressing room which opened off the bedroom, she found that the door at the other side of the room was not locked, so opened it carefully and gasped as she peered into the bedroom beyond.

Except for the fact that Mrs. Hodges saw to it that this room was kept as free from dust as was every other inch of the house, it stood just as Sir Percy had left it upon his hasty departure to escape his creditors. With so many other rooms from which to choose, Ariel had well nigh forgotten its existence, and certainly had no thought that anyone would look into it; otherwise, she would have given orders to have it locked.

A riding crop and a pair of gloves lay upon a table alongside some old sporting journals and two brushes, definitely masculine and overlooked in his hurried packing, were upon a small table at the bedside.

So excited by her find that she did not take the time to look into the wardrobe for the men's clothing she was certain would be hanging there, Myrtle came near to tumbling down the stairs in her haste to reach some of her bosom bows, to whisper her sensational news in their ears. There immediately occurred a near-epidemic of torn flounces as the others dashed upstairs to verify her story, for they knew that Myrtle was not above twisting the truth when it suited her purpose.

This time, the truth was far more exciting than anything she could have invented. The room was exactly as she had described it to them. Why, they asked one another, should a household which apparently consisted only of two ladies boast a bedroom which was beyond doubt a gentleman's room, and that room connected to Lady Ariel's? It could only mean –

"I wonder who he can be," the girls whispered, gazing at this evidence and giggling as each of them determined that she would be the fortunate one to learn the answer and confound her friends.

Such a deliciously naughty story as this was much too exciting to be kept; the girls told it to their mothers and to such friends as had not been fortunate enough to be present to view the find for themselves. It spread quickly throughout the *ton*, to be received with emotions varying from amusement to horror.

A married lady might be permitted to have lovers, as many as she might wish, as long as she handled her liaisons in a reasonably discreet manner. A widow, although she was permitted more freedom than an unmarried girl, ought to be more careful. And never should she have *his* room alongside her own for any curious person to see. There was nothing discreet in *such* behavior.

"I always thought that she was fast from the moment I saw her," Myrtle Soames said spitefully, remembering the loss of the gown – which she considered that Ariel had really stolen from her – as she recounted her discovery to her mother. Another mother might have given her daughter a scold for her prying, but Lady Soames did not.

"Fast is scarcely the proper word to use in describing such behavior," she declared, so impressed by the tale that she quite failed to notice that her daughter had emptied the entire dish of bonbons, lately banned from her diet in an attempt to reduce her size, into a serviette to be taken to her room for a forbidden treat. "*I* say that it is nothing short of scandalous. And you may depend upon it, my dear, I shall give her the cut direct should our paths chance to cross again."

She held by this decision and her example was followed by several of the other ladies to whom she had repeated her daughter's story, suitably embellished with her own opinions as to Lady Ariel's conduct.

Among the most outspoken in their condemnation of her ladyship was Mrs. Drummond Burrell, who insisted upon reminding her fellow Patronesses that *she* had known from the beginning that Lady Ariel was not worthy of admittance to Almack's. Since none of the other ladies had suggested that she should be received, such an attitude did little to improve relations in that group.

The rumor naturally had not been repeated in Ariel's hearing, nor had it come to the ears of anyone who was concerned with her welfare. She was much surprised, therefore, at the suddenly icy behavior of several ladies who had earlier expressed a desire for her friendship. The attitude of Mrs. Drummond

Burrell did not concern her in the least; she had always been aware of that lady's critical attitude toward her. Lady Soames' disdain was hardly noticed; as for the others, she could only think that they were volatile.

SEVEN

By far the greater number of Lady Ariel's acquaintances remained undisturbed when they heard the stories about her. Some of them declared that so charming a lady could not be guilty of such indiscretion. Others, such as Lady Jersey, shrugged them off as being unworthy of comment.

Scandal of one sort or another had hung about Sally Jersey's name for the greater part of her life. It had done her no harm and she doubted that it would harm Ariel. Her refusal to proffer vouchers to Almack's to her ladyship carried with it no criticism of Ariel's private life – as long as it remained private. She thought now that Ariel had been foolish, but had no intention of cutting her.

London's society thrived upon its scandals – the favourite *on-dit* of each new season must certainly be the discussion of who might have been the father of Lady So-and-So's latest child. Did it not bear a distinct resemblance to Lord Someone Else? If not that story, there was always the choice bit about the gentleman who had been spied sneaking out of some lady's window, her bedroom window, of course, just as her husband came in the front door. From the number of people who had *this* story to tell, it must be thought that half of the *ton* congregated in the streets at night to spy upon the other half.

Those who took the greatest interest in the rumors about Lady Ariel were certain gentlemen among her acquaintances, although they would have denied with great indignation that *they* were gossiping about her. Their discussions were much too serious, to them, to be given such a label.

Since her arrival in London, her ladyship had not appeared to give preference to any one gentleman more than another, but had allowed each of them in turn to escort her to different functions. Neither had she been seen in the company of anyone other than themselves. For a time, each of them regarded the others with suspicion, but enough cross-questioning convinced each of them that the lady's lover could not be of their number. Also, if he were, would he not have been objecting to the attentions paid to her by the others?

"W-well then, if it ain't one of us, who is it?" demanded Freddy Baine, a plump young gentleman whose boyish form and manner belied his six and twenty years. "W-we have never seen her w-with anyone else." The letter "W" had always caused him trouble, which had made him the victim of a great deal of chaffing at school and since.

"Perhaps he – whoever he may be – has been detained and will come to town later," his friend Tony Merchant ventured.

"Or it may be that they have quarreled," young Viscount Ridge said hopefully, helping himself to a pinch of snuff from his jewel-encrusted box. Grins spread across their faces as the trio considered the possibility of this.

"I believe that Ridge must have the right sow by the ear," Mr. Baine agreed. "And in that case –"

"The lady must certainly be lonely."

This led to a long discussion, much of it ribald, about ladies and their lovers and it was agreed at last that each of them would try his fortune with Lady Ariel.

No gentleman who considered himself to be worthy of the title would think of encroaching upon the preserves of another – husbands excepted, of course, for they were always fair

122

game. To do so would not only be unsporting, it could also prove to be dangerous if the other gentleman was a good shot. Still, if the lady happened to be free at the moment – well. It stood to reason that if she had lost one paramour, she would welcome another.

Other groups of young gentlemen, as well as some who were no longer so young nor so gentlemanly, discussed her ladyship with equal freedom. One of the latter was the Honourable Peter Soames, who had never made the least attempt to live up to his title. Unlike his sister-in-law and his niece, he had not the slightest desire to cut Lady Ariel for her indiscretion. He owned the greater part of his successes to the indiscretions of ladies.

Mr. Soames had just entered his fortieth year, but the marks of debauchery had erased his earlier tendency to handsomeness and had made him appear at least ten years older than he actually was. Since his brother, Baron Soames, was more than fifteen years his senior – with only sisters between them – and had no sons, his title would in time pass into Peter's possession, which would have made him quite a prize if his manners had matched his estate.

He was known, however, to boast openly of the number of husbands he had cuckolded, careful never to mention the ladies' names, but describing them in such intimate detail that there could be little doubt of their identities, especially to others who knew them quite well, if more discreetly. His few friends frequently declared that it was nothing short of miraculous that some jealous husband had not put a period to his existence; his many enemies said it was not miraculous but disastrous.

Although often coarse in his speech, he never mentioned his conquests in the presence of ladies, but some hints of these boasts were whispered into the ears of each matchmaking mama by her husband, and she would instantly forbid her daughters to have anything to do with such a libertine. Had his appearance been more prepossessing, such bans might have been circumvented by some of the more daring daughters; as it was, they were content to avoid him.

When he began to boast of the ease with which he expected to win over Lady Ariel, one of his cronies ventured the opinion that her ladyship might have kept that second bedroom as a memorial to her late husband. The comment sent Mr. Soames into coarse laughter.

"Never try to tell me that jade is mourning for anyone," he told them. "One has only to look at her to know that – her gowns, her manner of flaunting herself. Either she has quarrelled with her fancy man and has left him somewhere in the country or – what is more probable – he has tired of her and has taken himself off in search of more agreeable game."

Several gentlemen protested that he must be in error. It was most improbable that anyone could have tired of so delectable a creature as Lady Ariel appeared to be. Others were of the same opinion, but did not voice it, and when Mr. Soames declared, citing many examples in the coarsest way, that there was no female who would not prove boring after a man had become familiar with her wiles, all reluctantly agreed that he had a broader knowledge of such things than they. After all, it was evident to everyone that the lady gave no sign of mourning for anyone – either husband or lover.

As the talk raced about the town, the betting books of every gaming house in London, from the eminence of White's and Brooks' to the most rackety of the hells, held records of the wagers made by a number of gentlemen, each one of whom was confident that he would be the next to win her ladyship's affections.

It was not to be thought that such information as was making its way about the *ton* would fail to come to the ears of

Colonel McMahon, for he was forever on the lookout for such spicy bits, either on his own account or on behalf of his royal patron. He made careful inquiries about the lady and, after having the opportunity of viewing her, decided that for the moment she might be above his touch. Carrying the tales to the Regent's ears, he reflected that, even if caught, the Prince's attention would not be held forever and after that, his turn might come.

When he heard what McMahon had to say about the lovely Lady Ariel, the Regent reversed himself and sent word that he would honour Lady Willey's ball with his presence, in spite of having earlier declined the invitation. The colonel had ascertained that Lady Ariel would be one of the guests and the Regent thought this a good opportunity to see her for himself.

This decision upon the Prince's part threw Lady Willey, a creature of far less sense than sensibility, into such a positive flurry of excitement that it threatened to bring on an attack of the vapors. She was saved only by the coolness of her secretary, who was accustomed to such crises and set about making the necessary rearrangements.

From the viewpoint of any gentleman, even one with as many years of experience as the

Regent, Lady Ariel was certainly worth the attention she was receiving this evening. In her determination to make an unforgettable impression, she had demanded from Madame Josette a gown which would be different from all the others at the ball and Madame, throwing caution to the winds, designed one unlike any of her other creations – one which she had secretly hoped to see brought to life.

The result made her certain that, although not one female in one hundred could wear it with the elegance that Lady Ariel displayed, half the members of the *ton* would be at her door demanding similar gowns after seeing this one upon her ladyship.

Assuring Madame that their creation was what she had in mind and thanking her with enthusiasms, Ariel nonetheless, found herself blushing when she looked into her mirror, and was driven to defense of the gown only by Clarissa's scandalized comments and Parsons' disapproval, which, while remaining unspoken, was no less evident.

"Ariel, how can you think of appearing at a ball in something like *that?*" her cousin demanded.

"Don't be such a widgeon, Clare," Ariel said with some impatience, for she was trying to reassure herself as well as her cousin. "Actually, this gown exposes much less of

127

my – bosom – than half of the gowns which will be worn this evening."

"I know that, but –" Clarissa's objection faded, but Ariel knew what she meant.

It was only that the gown made her *feel* so bare. Vaguely Grecian in its design, it fastened by a knot tied upon her right shoulder, leaving the left shoulder and both arms uncovered, and the gold tissue clung to her body in a most revealing manner. It ended above her ankles, revealing her sandals, also Grecian in design, whose gold thongs crisscrossed to tie somewhere above the gown's hem.

Within the sandals, her feet were bare and her toenails had been gilded. Her fingernails as well, some of the shocked matrons noticed. It was true that, upon occasions, some of the more daring ladies would paint their toenails, allowing them to be glimpsed only now and then under the edge of a longer gown.

No *lady*, however, even if she had become so lost to propriety as to appear in public without gloves, would think of painting her fingernails in so gaudy a color. Unaware that Ariel was merely following Josette's advice in this matter, they told one another that it was the sort of thing one might expect from the widow, and wondered what sort of disgraceful behavior she might exhibit next.

A tiara of topaz nestled before the black

curls piled across the top of her head and long earrings of matching stones almost brushed her shoulders. She had hesitated about wearing a necklace, then decided against doing so, believing that the effect of the gown would be lessened – even if a necklace, slight as it was, would have made her feel less uncovered. As well as anyone in the room, she was aware that her appearance was startling, almost barbaric.

Antoine had advised her to have her eyebrows slightly plucked and she had suffered through the ordeal, but admitted that their smoother shape suited her. Her brows and lashes were as black as her hair and there was no necessity for darkening them as many of the ladies did. She had not yet succumbed to the vogue of painting her face, but had reddened her lips tonight.

At her side when they entered the ballroom, Clarissa looked more demure than usual in a bergere gown of a blue slightly lighter than the color of her eyes and with her golden curls gleaming in the candlelight. There were many present, especially some of the shyer young gentlemen, who found her quiet beauty more attractive than her cousin's sophistication, and she did not lack for partners.

By far the greater number of the beaux, however, flocked about Ariel's golden form and she found herself solicited for dance after dance. Unaware of what was being said about her, she was astonished that so many of her partners seemed to be determined to coax her out into the garden or into one of the discreetly dim little rooms which her ladyship had thoughtfully provided for assignations among her guests.

It was not her habit to carry her flirtations to such lengths and she was happy to find that another partner was always at hand to claim her for the next dance, so that she could evade the suggestion that they leave the floor without causing any ill feelings.

Unless she was mistaken, many of these who began their praises by calling her "Golden One," "Vision," or – in one case – "Golden Goddess," followed up these salutations with remarks which were warmer than she was accustomed to hearing. Then she told herself that it was doubtless that she was not yet accustomed to London ways. Many gentlemen – and ladies, too, she had discovered – were given to making remarks which would have been considered quite shocking at home.

In time, she told herself, she would no longer give any notice to such things. She had wished to come to London; therefore she must adapt herself to its ways. Perhaps, too, she had invited some of their comments by her costume tonight. She had wanted to be daring, to be original. Had she gone beyond the limits of what was permissible, given them the impression that she was the sort who would welcome liberties? If any gentleman presumed that, he must be corrected at once.

As another partner appeared to request her to stand up with him, the music broke off in mid-strain and an agitated Lady Willey rushed to her side.

"Lady Ariel, if you please," she gasped and began to lead the girl almost at a run in the direction of the newest arrival, an unusually corpulent gentleman, well past his youth and clad in a coat of vivid pink velvet above pale primrose knitted breeches which appeared to be stretched nearly to the bursting point. It seemed to Ariel that a large part of the company was fawning upon him.

"Who is that?" she asked, trying to move more slowly for Lady Willey was almost pulling her off her feet. Her hostess gave her a shocked glance and whispered, "The Prince Regent."

Entirely overcome by the fact that Royalty had expressed an especial interest in having one of her guests presented – and that one the (nearly) notorious Lady Ariel Laurence – she continued to hurry the girl along to the spot where he was standing and exclaimed in one breath, "Your Highness, may I present Lady Ariel Laurence?"

Ariel sank into a deep curtsy, struggling to suppress a giggle when she heard the ominous creaking as the Regent bent to take her hand. She believed that he was actually wearing corsets!

Taking her silence to mean that the lady was overcome by the honour of being presented to him, which doubtless would have been the truth if she had not been under the necessity of fighting down the laughter which would certainly have insulted him, the Regent said kindly, as he drew her to her feet:

"Lady Ariel, instead of dancing, which I find that I do not enjoy as greatly as I once did, I wonder if you would be kind enough to stroll about with me for a time?" This was an untruth, for he did like to dance, but he had something other than dancing in mind at the moment.

Ariel disliked missing even a single dance, as she had spent a great deal of money on dancing lessons for herself and Clarissa, and enjoyed stepping about the floor in the figures of any dance. However, she supposed that she could not say anything of the sort to the Regent, who must be humored. Doubtless dancing was fatiguing to him. She had heard that many fat men were excellent dancers, but surely not when they were *this* fat and this old.

She nodded agreement to his wishes and allowed him to tuck her hand within the crook of his arm before he signaled to the musicians to resume playing and began to lead her about the room, speaking genially to a number of the people. Since they all bowed or curtsied to him, Ariel could not help the feeling that this courtesy was extended to her as well.

An excited buzz of conversation sprang up behind them as it was noticed that their route was taking them directly toward the doors which led to the terrace.

As a rule, the Regent preferred to choose his mistresses from among the ladies of his own age or perhaps a trifle older; he liked the plump, motherly type for, despite his more than fifty years, there was still much of the spoilt boy in him and he felt more comfortable with older ladies. However, he was no more averse than any other man to savoring the attractions of a beautiful face and form.

This young widow possessed both, and, according to the rumors that McMahon had heard, she was between lovers at the moment. Lonely ladies, he had found, were often the most ardent.

He did not doubt that she would be willing, even eager, to accept his attentions for a time;

after all, it was no light thing to have the First Gentleman of Europe for a lover. If she was as pleasing as she looked, she might keep his attention for a long time. She could prove to be an agreeable change from his elderly ladies. Also, she was wealthy, or so he had been told, which meant that he need not go further into debt to provide her with trinkets.

Notwithstanding the fact that he had long since ceased to be the Prince Florizel whose face and form had fluttered the hearts of the ladies of an earlier generation, the Prince still knew how to charm a young female with his conversation. He asked for her opinion of London, what sights she had seen and what sort of entertainments she had found here, as they strolled down the terrace steps and along the pathway.

Engrossed in what he was saying, which was such a pleasant change from many of the rather coarse remarks which had been poured into her ears for the past hour or so, Ariel was not aware for several moments of the plump arm which had been slipped about her waist. When she noticed it, she took a quick step forward to avoid its encirclement and said, a bit breathlessly, "Your Highness —"

"Now," he said soothingly, catching both her hands and attempting to draw her closer, "You must forget that I am the Regent."

It did not occur to him that if he was *not* the Regent, most ladies would not look in his direction. "Just think of me as one of your admirers. After all, there is nothing wrong with a bit of cuddling and a kiss or two between a man and a woman, is there?" Releasing her hands, he now used both arms to encircle her waist.

Ariel continued to try to pull free from his embrace, wondering what she could do. It was out of the question to slap the face of the country's ruler as she might have done if any other fat old man had dared to take such liberties. She would have to think of something quickly for he was now holding her so tightly that several of his medals were pricking her skin and his stays were pressing into her with cruel force as he attempted to reach her lips.

Bending backward as far as his grasp would permit and turning her head aside so that his mouth merely grazed her ear, she gasped, "Your Highness – you must not – that is, *I* must not. You honor me – but – but I am not free –"

Releasing her so suddenly that she almost fell and had to stagger backward to remain on her feet, the Prince demanded, "You mean that there is someone else? I was informed that your husband is dead."

He was well aware that an angry husband could cause a scandal if he was not properly handled. Fortunately, he had never had that problem, but it had happened to several of his acquaintances and the results had been disastrous. Doubtless there were even some men who would not consider it an honor to know that their wives were preferred by the Regent.

"Yes –" he was happy to hear her say. "He is – but –"

It would be a great comfort at this time, Ariel thought, if she could claim a husband who was very much alive, but everyone had been told that she was a widow. Still, his question had provided her with a solution. She must allow him to believe that there was another man, one who would be very jealous – someone far different from poor, dull Henry, who would never be considered a rival by the Regent.

She had invented a husband; why could she not invent a lover as well? Most of the ladies of the *ton* seemed to have them, so there would be nothing so disgraceful about that.

"Not my husband – but – someone else. Someone who would be quite angry if he learned of this. I could not bear it if I should be the cause of trouble between you."

So there *was* another man, the Regent thought. Someone who was important enough that he might cause unpleasant talk if this episode became known. Damn McMahon! Why could he not have checked more carefully into the lady's status before he offered her to his master? How dared he place his Prince in so foolish a position? Still, it had happened; now one must make the best of the situation.

He raised Ariel's hand to his lips and said as genially as he could manage, "I must envy the gentleman who has so loyal a sweetheart as you. May I know his name?"

What ought she to tell him now? She did not dare to give him the name of a real person. It would not be right to involve anyone else in her lies; also, that individual would be certain to expose her fabrication the moment he learned of it. Nor could she invent a name. The Regent was certain to know everyone of importance and would be aware that she had lied to him. He would feel that she had insulted him, and who knew what the result might be?

"He is away from London at the moment," she improvised. "And I do not think he would wish me to speak of the connection – even to Your Highness – until he is at my side."

"Then we certainly shall not do so," the Regent promised, tucking her hand within his arm once more and patting it paternally, then turning so that they might stroll back to the ballroom, where he released her to a gentleman who was eager to dance with her.

Not one of Lady Willey's guests had missed the fact that the Regent had taken Lady Ariel into the gardens, but none had made more careful note of the shortness of time they had been gone than had Mr. Soames. Seeing that the Prince, after relinquishing her ladyship to another, had spoken briefly with his hostess and had then departed, showing every sign of having been disappointed, he was quick to draw his own conclusions as to what had happened in the garden.

"If the doxy was going to be taken under the Regent's protection, he would have taken her with him at once for he is not the sort to put off his pleasures," he said to himself. "And certainly, no female in London – in all of England for that matter – would be foolish enough to refuse such an offer. Therefore, he did not make it, was not pleased with her for some reason. But it may be that I have seen something in the lady that our Prince has overlooked."

Edging out a number of other eager partners, he caught Lady Ariel's hand just as she was about to place it upon the arm of a callow youth, and drew her out into the waltz which was just beginning. Ariel looked up at

138

him in astonishment, for she did not believe that he had been presented to her. However, with so many young handsome men among the guests, she might well have missed one who must be nearly the Regent's age, although not so fat.

"Have we met, sir?" she asked.

"Only now, my Golden One, but it is not yet too late," he said and, seeing the beaux who were impatiently waiting to claim her when this dance had ended, maneuvered her about so that, when the music stopped, they were beside the terrace door. Before any of the others could reach them, he had swept her out through the door.

Oh, not again, Ariel thought wildly and began, "Sir, we ought not –" but he had his arm tightly about her waist and was half leading, half dragging her down the steps and toward a secluded nook which had served him well in the past.

"There is no need to behave so coyly with me," he said with a laugh which grated upon her ears. "Come, offer me the same inducements you gave to our fat Prince. You may be certain that I shall not despise them as he did."

"You insult me, sir," Ariel gasped, struggling vainly against the arm which imprisoned her. She attempted to kick at him, but the thin Grecian sandals had almost no effect and she nearly lost her balance in making the attempt. If only she were swearing her stout country boots – *then* she could make him set her free.

"Insult you? No. I find you bewitching." She could smell the spirits on his breath as he spoke.

They had reached the spot he had in mind and drew her from the pathway into the sheltered nook. This was a far more dangerous man than the Regent, she thought. No talk of a jealous but absent lover would deter him; in fact, it might well give him an added incentive to conquer her. It was clear that she must depend upon herself to get free of him.

"You must let me go," she said with as much authority as she could muster, but despite all her efforts to sound authoritative, her voice shook and he only laughed again.

"Free you? Not until we have come to know each other much better."

One arm still held her fast while his other hand fumbled at the knot which fastened her gown at the shoulder. If he succeeded in untying it, the entire gown would fall off, which was certainly what he had in mind. The reek of spirits was so much stronger now that his face was close to hers and was mixed with other, less pleasant smells upon his breath, so that she felt that she must surely swoon; she fought against it, knowing that he was doubtless the sort of man who would take pleasure in ravishing her before she regained consciousness.

The scruples which had prevented her from striking the Prince did not deter her now and, even though her left arm was pinioned at her side, her right was free. She doubted, however, that a mere slap would stop him, so she doubled her fist and brought it down with all her force across the bridge of his nose.

Mr. Soames howled and released her, grasping for his handkerchief to stanch the spurt of blood before it ruined his finery. Ariel darted away, running up the path to the ballroom door. Then, realizing that it must give rise to a great deal of gossip if she should burst into the room in such a panic-stricken manner, she drew herself together and entered with as much dignity as she could manage.

Fortunately, her tussle with Peter Soames had not been sufficient to disarrange her hair and he had not succeeded in his object of untying the shoulder knot of her gown, so she showed no outward sign of what had occurred. She was much disturbed in spirit, however, that two gentlemen, if one could give the libertine from whom she had just escaped such a title, had made such advances to her within the hour, and determined that they ought to leave as soon as she could find Clarissa.

As she was searching for her cousin among the dancers, Freddie Baine approached and begged the honor of escorting her to supper. She had no appetite, but she could see that Clarissa would be engaged in this dance for a time and, looking at the boyish face before her, decided that perhaps he might be trusted. Still, she said, "It would be my pleasure, Mr. Baine. But I must insist that we go to the supper room only. I do *not* wish to go out onto the terrace."

"Oh no, Lady Ariel, I would not presume to suggest anything of that sort," the young gentleman protested quickly, shocked that she should be so blunt. In truth, he would have liked nothing better than to try his fortune with the lady this evening, for he had wagered rather more than he could afford upon his ability to win her.

He had seen her earlier, however, being led away into the garden by the Regent and had noticed that she had been almost carried away by Mr. Soames. Since he could match neither the rank of the first nor the forcefulness of the second, he decided that, for the moment, an attitude of respectful admiration might serve him best.

He found her a seat in the supper room, then rushed off to obtain a plate filled with lobster patties and enough creams to satisfy half a dozen ladies. When Ariel laughed and protested that she could not eat more than a small part of what he had brought, he volunteered to help her and ate from her plate with much the air of a small boy at his first grownup tea, which did much to put her at her ease. As he ate, he tried to lead her to talk of her life before she came to London.

"There is nothing worth the telling," Ariel said positively determined that no one must ever know about Sylvester and his nip-farthing ways. "We lived a very quiet life in the country."

"I understand – of course you were in mourning," he agreed and Ariel, who had a tendency to forget about her "soldier husband" unless reminded, was quick to say,

"Yes – yes, I was – but he would not have wished me to mourn him forever. In fact, he all but ordered me not to do so, if he should not return from the Peninsula, which I am sorry to say is what happened."

She had certainly put off her mourning with a vengeance, he thought, eying her golden gown and the flashing jewelry. He wondered if she was sorry or happy to be rid of the man. "I presume that he must have been a neighbor," he went on. "A childhood sweetheart, perhaps, for you must have married young. And until you came to London, then, you had never met any of the *ton?*"

His question was posed so ingenuously that she had no qualms about answering – as long as he did not delve too deeply into the details of her "marriage."

"No – never." Then, with the memory of that fleeting encounter at the posting house, she added, "Except for Lord Dexter, of course."

"Dexter?" His ears pricked up at the name, for it was known that Dexter was frequently out of the city, ostensibly to visit his estates – but who knew what other visits he might make? "You know him well, do you?"

"Oh no – I must not let it appear that I am a friend. But he was kind to me."

"Kind? Dexter?" The thought brought a whoop of laughter. "No one has ever accused him of being kind."

Recalling how a careless word from the nobleman had persuaded the reluctant landlord not to put them out and how he had given up his own room so that they might have the best, Ariel said a bit stiffly, "*I* found him to be so."

Mr. Baine's excitement was so great that he

found his appetite was no longer tempted by the array of rich creams and he could scarcely wait until the strains of the music summoned them back to the dance floor.

A group of gentlemen surrounded Ariel at once, but she put them all aside, for she had spied Clarissa. A bit surprised to learn that her cousin should wish to leave at so early an hour, the younger girl nonetheless made no demur and they bade their hostess a good night. As the ladies left the room, Mr. Baine gathered a group of his friends together to impart his startling discovery.

"I know who he is," he declared.

"You know who who is?" Tony Merchant asked, causing Viscount Ridge to protest.

"Damnation, Tony, must you make sounds like an owl? It makes my flesh creep. And what are you chortling about, Freddie?"

"Lady Ariel's lover. I know who he is." He had all their attention now and he prolonged the suspense until the others were beginning to make threats before he said, "Dexter."

"Dexter? I cannot believe it," Mr. Merchant scoffed.

"No more could I, at first. And she did not admit it in so many words, but said she had known no one but him before she came to London, that she would not claim to be a 'friend,' and that he had been very kind to her. What else could she have meant?"

All agreed that he must have the right of it, then the Viscount said, "Dexter returns to town within a few days, as he is certainly promised to the Regent's dinner party. Then we shall discover whether the *affaire* is still current, or if someone else has a chance with her. I, for one, would not fight Dexter for any woman on earth."

EIGHT

Mindful as always of their well-being, the fourth Earl of Dexter tooled his team of chestnuts carefully along the road in the direction of London. Randall Augustus Frederick Vernon could race with the best of the Corinthians and had, time after time, won large wagers from those among his friends who considered themselves to be superior whips, but he cared too much for his cattle to spring them when there was no need for him to do so, and especially over such roads as these.

With the exception of the first day, when the attractions of a fair charmer had caused him to leave the city much later than he had planned to do, and the subsequent throwing of a shoe by one of his leaders had further delayed him so that he was forced to spend the night at an inn which could be dubbed only passable, his journey had proven satisfactory upon every count.

He had paid visits to several of his estates, finding, as he had quite expected to do, that everything was in perfect order. There was never any need for the earl to listen to the complaints of his tenants, or to discover that rents had not been collected. His factors were well aware that their positions were forfeit if the earl should arrive unexpectedly, as he frequently did, to find anything amiss, and their records were always ready for his approval.

Dexter had discovered several prime bits of blood to add to his already extensive stables and had spent time in the homes of some old friends, engaging in flirtations with any of the willing wives, but carefully avoiding entanglements with any unmarried girls whose families might wish to make him an addition to their number. Since he always conducted his liaisons discreetly, there was no question of his being unwelcome in any home he chose to visit.

With all of these matters behind him, he had sent his groom ahead of him to London, telling him that he could manage for the next several days on his own. Knowing well enough where his master was bound, the servant made no comment, only gave him a cheeky grin, which would have earned him a severe reprimand if he had not been in the service of the third Earl and had known Master Randall since he was in short coats.

Seeing the grin, the earl only growled, "Oh, go to the devil, Charles," which earned him another grin and a wink before the man left.

The earl's next stop was at a small house on the outskirts of Bristol, where a most obliging piece of muslin had enjoyed his protection for some time. This interlude was such a pleasant one that only the remembrance that he was expected in London for the Prince Regent's dinner made him take his leave.

He had been tempted to remain one more day, enjoying her company, but that would have meant that he would have had to push his cattle to arrive home on time, and even the most enticing ladybird could not oblige him to do that. After complaining in a mild way that she might have known that he thought more of his chestnuts than he did of her, and begging him to return to her as soon as he might, the dove sent him on his way with so many kisses and protestations of her fidelity that he could not help but wonder if she entertained others in his absence.

"I cannot blame her if she does," he told himself, "for she is certainly a full-blooded wench and I see her so seldom. And who could expect fidelity from one of her kind?"

If he discovered that this was so, he would not hesitate to put her aside, but with regret, for he had found her lovemaking most enjoyable; too, she was intelligent enough to be able to offer him companionship as well as passion and she was less greedy than some of her predecessors.

Arriving at his London house, he relinquished the team to the care of his groom, swearing good-naturedly at the man for volunteering to ask if he had had an enjoyable time. The moment he entered the house, footmen appeared to relieve him of his hat, gloves, and riding coat, and his butler presented him with the messages which had arrived during his absence. He mounted to his bedchamber, certain that his valet would have his bath awaiting him, for here, too, the servants were accustomed to anticipate his wishes.

Even so accomplished a whip as the earl could not fail to find the journey a bit tiring and he was happy to soak himself for some time in the hot bath, emerging to attire himself in a frilled shirt and the calflength evening trousers which had been made popular by Beau Brummell. Although the Beau had fallen from favor and had been forced to flee abroad to escape his creditors, the styles which he had set were still followed by many members of the *ton*.

When he had meticulously arranged his cravat in the style which was beginning to be copied by the would-be dandies who had labeled it the Dexter fall, his valet helped him into the snugly fitting coat of corbeau-coloured superfine and handed him the magnificent emerald ring which had belonged to his father and was the only piece of jewelry the earl would wear. As his master went down the stairs, the valet gathered up the discarded clothing, thinking smugly that no one at Carlton House this evening, and especially not its owner, would be able to hold a candle to the earl.

As Dexter entered the building, his host came to meet him, clad in an enormous coat of mustard yellow satin, clustered with many jewels and worn above violet inexpressibles. After his disagreement with the Beau, the Regent refused to take any advice in the choice of his clothing, relying only upon his own taste, which was much too flamboyant for a man of his girth. Looking at the unmarred smoothness of Dexter's coat, the Prince demanded,

"Did you get that coat from Weston?"

"Certainly, sir. I never allow anyone else to cut coats for me, as you know."

"Well, he made this for me, and I cannot understand why he always fits you so well and me so poorly," the Prince complained. Nearly every member of the Regent's set had heard this remark time after time. He must have known the answer as well as they; but even if he did not, none of them would remind him that if they allowed their poundage to match his, their coats would not fit so well, either.

The Prince, whose appetite for rich food and drink was as great as all his other appetites, indulged himself upon every occasion and took less exercise with every stone added to his weight. Dexter, on the other hand, ate and drank sparingly.

He hunted in season and rode almost every morning, no matter what enticements had kept him awake the night before. Also, he worked out with great regularity, either with the foils or in John Jackson's famous saloon, where he had been one of the few privileged to stand up regularly with the Gentleman and one of the even smaller number who had been able to land a flush hit over Jackson's guard, an act that gentleman explained away with the remark that he was no longer so young as he had been and that it would never have happened ten years before.

The result of this combination of moderation and exercise was that the only trouble the great Weston had in cutting the earl's coat was to attempt to disguise some of his well-developed muscles. Even in another twenty years, when he attained the Regent's present age, it was most unlikely that he would have any tendency toward obesity.

Knowing that any further discussion of their clothing would only serve to increase the Regent's sense of being ill-treated, Dexter turned the subject, complimenting the Prince upon the latest painting he had purchased. In matters of art, the Prince's taste was unsurpassed by anyone in London and his collections of paintings, miniatures, glass, and china were the envy of his friends as well as the despair of the government who received the bills.

From time to time as the evening wore on, Dexter received the impression that Prinny had been looking at him with a sort of uneasiness. Since he was unable to think of any reason for his, he decided that either it was his imagination or, as frequently happened, the Prince had eaten something which disagreed with him. When the other guests began to take their leave, however, the Prince signaled him to remain behind and, when they were alone, said,

"Dexter, despite the slight difference in our ages, you know that I have always considered you to be an especial friend."

"And I am honored at having your friendship," the earl replied, thinking that only Prinny could call a difference of a score of years a slight one. He also wondered what the Prince had meant by that remark and reflected that the Royal friendship could be withdrawn in a moment of pique, as poor Brummell had discovered.

"You – you must realize that I would never knowingly have – you had never mentioned –" It was so unlike the usually garrulous Prince to be at a loss for words that Dexter prompted,

"I had never mentioned what?"

"Not what, man. Who. The lady."

Dexter stared at him, trying to puzzle the meaning of his words and the Prince, misreading his expression, began to laugh somewhat nervously. Lady Ariel had told him that her lover would be angry if he learned that the Prince had made advances to her; and now that he had been told that the man was Dexter, he knew she had told the truth. The earl was known to have a devilishly hot temper and might not draw the line at calling out even his Prince over such a matter.

Of course, such a meeting would never be permitted to take place, even if duels were not now against the law, but he could imagine the scandal if the challenge was issued. In his scandal-ridden life, there were some things which the Regent felt *must* not be allowed to happen, and to be publicly embroiled over the favors of a female was one of them.

Even worse than that – Dexter might assault him physically, believing that the Prince would not risk the publicity which would result from having him punished for what he had done. He looked at Dexter's muscular form and shuddered.

"Oh, she was discreet enough about your acquaintance, I can assure you," he said quickly. "Not even to her Prince would she reveal your name; said that she believed you would prefer that she did not mention it until you had come to town. But word gets around; you know how it is – it is absolutely impossible to keep any sort of a secret in London. It seems that the very winds carry the news. I only wish that you will believe me. I would never have said anything at all to Lady Ariel if I had the least idea –"

"Lady Ariel?" Dexter repeated, more

confused than before by the Prince's explanation.

The Prince laughed, not quite so nervously this time, and clapped him upon the shoulder. Either her ladyship had thought that the encounter was not worth the mentioning or else she had made so light of it that the earl had decided not to be angry with him after all.

"I must tell you that I envy you your choice, my boy, for she appears delightful. I can only hope that you will bear me no ill will for having been somewhat taken with her myself."

"Certainly not, sir," the earl replied and, since it seemed that the Prince had said all he intended to upon the subject, soon made his *adieux*. As he headed his horses toward his own house, he wondered if it could be possible that Prinny's mind was beginning to go as his father's had done, for not one word of the Prince's strange conversation had made the least sense to him.

However, it seemed that wherever he appeared the next day, from White's to Manton's to Cribb's Parlours, every friend he met made a point of speaking to him about Lady Ariel Laurence, chaffing him for allowing such a dasher to come up to London without him to keep an eye upon her and slyly questioning whether the fact that she had come alone meant that the two of them had quarreled.

"I hope you will say that you did so, because some of the rest of us may have a chance," his friend David Mortimer commented, while someone else complained,

"It ain't fair that Dexter, who already has so much, should have the lady, too."

Bit by bit, he pieced out the fact that a certain young widow, newly arrived in London, who must – from the comments he had heard about her – be a lightskirt, despite the title she claimed, had been telling everyone that he was her paramour. At last he understood what was behind Prinny's remarks and his nervousness; doubtless the Prince's eye had fallen upon her and she had used *his* name to discourage the Regent. He could not understand that; such a creature should be only too happy to find Royal favor.

Several times he opened his mouth to deny that he had any knowledge of the imposter, then closed it again. The "lady" had done her work too well. Any denial on his part would only expose him to more chaffing. His friends would believe that he was trying to keep the liaison a secret, despite the creature's indiscreet talk.

Make him a laughingstock among his

friends, would she, he thought wrathfully, determined that he would seek out this jade, whoever she might be, and make her admit her lies. How dared she trade upon his name to make a reputation for herself?

When one of his friends remarked slyly that certainly everyone would be looking forward to seeing them together at Mrs. Harriet Sloane's rout that evening, Dexter replied somewhat grimly that he planned to surprise the lady by appearing unannounced, as he had not yet apprised her of his return to the city.

"Trying to catch her out in a flirtation with someone else – no doubt about that," said the gossips, none of whom had failed to notice Dexter's grimness. Each of them congratulated himself that *he* had not yet become involved with her. Still, if all was not well between the two, those who had hoped they might supplant Dexter in Lady Ariel's affections took heart; there might yet be a chance to do so.

It would certainly come as a surprise to the creature, he thought, when he faced her down before all that company and forced her to admit her chicanery. He would choke the truth out of her if it was necessary. He had no doubt that an invitation to the Sloane affair might be found somewhere in the stack of correspondence which he had tossed upon his desk without a glance; but even without it, Mrs. Sloane's door, like almost every other door in London, would be open to the Earl of Dexter.

Mrs. Sloane squeaked with pleasure when the handsome red-haired nobleman presented himself to her that evening, apologizing for having appeared without an invitation.

"In truth, Harriet," he said, "I have not been home long enough to look through my letters to see if one had been sent."

"It does not matter in the least, my *dear* Dexter," she cooed, the purple plumes in her improbably orange hair bobbing as she curtsied to him. "You know that you are always welcome in my house."

She would have welcomed him with even greater warmth if he had called when she was alone, but she knew such a call was too much for her to hope for – just now.

"Had I the slightest indication that you would have returned to London so soon – not that any time you are away is not too long for those of us who miss you – you *know* that an invitation would have been sent to you, of all people. But Lady Ariel gave me no – that is we had no indication that you would be returning so soon."

She knew that she was repeating herself, babbling about nothings, but astonishment at

158

his arrival must be blamed for this. Leaning forward, so that he might have the best view of her décolletage, she peered past him, asking archly, "You are not alone, surely?"

"For the moment," he said, seething with anger.

Not only were the bucks talking about him and the "lady" – he did not doubt that her title was as false as everything else about her – but now it seemed that the hens were cackling as well. He should have expected that, of course. If there was any gossip about, they would have it at their tongues' ends. All the more reason for giving the jade a setdown she would long remember.

"Tonight is in the nature of a surprise," he explained.

"A most pleasant surprise, I am certain – for someone," she tittered, hoping that, in truth, it *would* be pleasant. Like almost everyone else in London, she was aware that Lord Dexter's temper matched his hair and if he took violent exception to some of the gentlemen who flocked about Lady Ariel like flies about a honey-pot, Mrs. Sloane hoped that it would not be during her party.

On the other hand, such a confrontation, although many would condemn it as being in the worst of taste, would make her rout the most talked-about affair in weeks, so it might not be such an unfortunate thing if it did happen.

Dexter passed on into the room, greeting his friends with a fixed smile, his fury increasing with every knowing glance he intercepted. He had never minded the publicity which appeared to surround all his amours – when they *were* his amours. It was only the idea of this unknown jade claiming him.

He became aware that Lady Soames was casting furious glances in his direction and his spirits took a sudden lift. For months, he had been successfully avoiding the net which she had been spreading in his direction. Simply because her ladyship and his Aunt Myrtle had been bosom-bows a quarter of a century earlier and his aunt had later stood godmother to that muffin-faced Soames chit, Lady Soames thought that she could snare him for her son-in-law.

If "Lady Ariel," with her false claim, had put a spoke in *that* wheel, he thought that he might be inclined to deal with her a bit more leniently than he had first intended. Not that he would let her go entirely unpunished; she must learn that she could not make free with his name in such a fashion.

Ariel and Clarissa had been a bit late in arriving at the rout. In fact, Ariel was a bit uneasy about her costume for this evening, remembering the unpleasant events which had occurred at Lady Willey's ball. What she was doing tonight, she thought, was actually more daring than that, but it was nothing more than many other ladies had been practicing for some time.

Clarissa had not seen her cousin before they donned their cloaks to leave home and when they first arrived, she had been concerned with adjusting the drape of her own gown of pale blue crape embroidered with silver rosebuds. As they entered the ballroom, she fell several steps behind her cousin as she still did at times, for she had not grown accustomed to being in such exalted company, then gasped with dismay as she watched Ariel being led out for the first dance.

Ariel had heard that many ladies dampened their petticoats, but, never having seen how it was done and feeling that Parsons would be shocked if asked for advice on such a subject, she had as usual acted impulsively. Wishing to do a thorough job of it, she had actually soaked the cloth, so that beneath the sheer claret-colored silk of her gown, she might as well have been wearing nothing. There were at least a dozen other dampened petticoats about the room, but Clarissa did not notice them. To think that *Ariel* would behave in so immodest a fashion –

Moving through the steps of the country dance, Ariel was already regretting that she had acted so boldly. The wet muslin of the petticoat hung clammily to her skin, feeling most unpleasant and preventing her from moving as freely as she might wish. Not for the world, however, would she have admitted her discomfort, but laughed and chatted with her entranced partner each time the pattern of the dance brought them together, as if everything was going as it should.

Standing to one side and watching the dancers, it took Dexter only a short time to gather, from the glances which were cast from him to the female and from the muttered comments, that this was the creature who was boasting of having snared him. He grinned appreciatively as he studied her moving through the figures of the dance.

The dampened petticoat revealed that she had a superb figure, which was more than could be said for several of the others who had essayed the fashion, and her face was beautiful as well. She was undoubtedly a bold piece and he decided that, instead of denouncing her at once, he would enjoy himself with her for a time; he could always make her admit that she had lied about attaching him when the jest had palled.

Waiting until the musicians began to play

a waltz, he stepped forward and shouldered aside several of those who had been crowding about the Lady – many of whom were quick to efface themselves when they became aware of his identity – and saying, "Mine, I believe, gentlemen," in a tone which warned away the others. He slipped a firm arm about her waist and drew her onto the floor without allowing her an opportunity to accept or decline his partnership.

Ariel stiffened in his embrace, but had little choice except to follow his lead. He was behaving as ruthlessly as the man who had taken her into the garden at Lady Willey's, but this was a much younger gentleman – a stranger.

Wondering if all the gentlemen had put aside their manners, Ariel looked up to meet the mocking gaze in his amber eyes. There was something about those eyes – reminding her of those of an animal – something, too, about the dark red hair which seemed to strike a familiar note. She had met so many people during her weeks in London that it was impossible for her to remember all of them. Still, it occurred to her that this was a gentleman who would not have been easy to forget.

Certainly she would have remembered if she had danced with him before, for there

163

was an arrogance in the way he had captured her for this waltz which was unusual. Also, his dancing was much better than that of many of the other partners she had favored. Would he think her gauche if she asked his name? Perhaps so; it might be the habit of some of the ladies of the *ton* to accept, even to welcome, such behavior from a stranger. If so, she would prefer to follow the mode, but was overcome by her curiosity.

"Have we met before?" she asked.

It was the same question that she had posed to the man who had dragged her into the garden, and whose name she now knew to be Peter Soames, but the result was quite different. Instead of indulging in gallantry, this gentleman threw back his head and laughed so heartily that heads turned in their direction; everyone wondering what had occurred to amuse Dexter and his lady-love. Had she perhaps been boasting of her conquests in his absence or making sport of those who had aspired to her attention? One thing was certain; there was no trouble between the pair.

Thinking that, for all he intended to give her a setdown, he must admire the jade for her daring, Dexter said, "I have been told that we have."

This only confused Ariel the more.

Certainly, *he* ought to know if they had been introduced, but why did he not tell her what the occasion had been, as anyone else would have done? Could it be that he was absentminded or was it that he met so many girls that he could not remember which was which?

Something in the manner in which he looked down at her was most disturbing and she hoped that he was not thinking of sweeping her off to the terrace or to some secluded spot. She was not certain that he could be put off as easily as Mr. Soames had been.

When the dance ended, however, he returned her to the knot of her admirers, raised her hand to his lips and said, "Until later, my love," before striding away.

The other gentlemen were quick to crowd about her as they had done before, demanding that she choose her next partner, since it had been made clear that his lordship was not intending to object if the lady *danced* with others. They would be careful, however, to let him see that they did not wish more from her than a dance or two.

Ariel refused all the offers. Between the discomfort caused by her damp petticoat and the disturbing sensation the stranger had aroused in her – had his last remark been mere gallantry or the threat he had made it sound? – Ariel spoke no more than the truth when she pleaded the beginning of a migraine. Collecting Clarissa from her crowd of admirers, she beat a hasty retreat from the house.

Clarissa noticed that her cousin was unusually silent this evening, but she had a matter of her own that she was wondering how best to broach to Ariel. Absorbed in her own thoughts, she did not venture to mention her cousin's bold attire and, in fact, gave little heed to what was going on about them until Ariel exclaimed, "Lord Dexter!"

"Who?" Clarissa roused herself to peer out of the carriage window, thinking Ariel was calling her attention to some passing acquaintance and wondering how she could have recognized anyone when the street about them was so dark.

"Lord Dexter – you remember, Clare, when we were on our way to London, the gentleman who forced the landlord to let us have a room. In fact, he gave us the one which had been given him. That is who it was. I thought I ought to know him when we danced."

"Oh –" Her cousin was scarcely listening, uninterested. "I should not have remembered him."

"Nor did I, until this moment, although I was certain that I had seen him somewhere. 'Twas that red hair – and his arrogant manner – which made me think I knew him. Nor would I have thought that he remembered me – you know what a complete dowd I looked at the inn – but he laughed a great deal when I asked if we had met, so he must remember. But he could not tell me. I vow, Clare, I believe there is something odd about his lordship."

Back in Mrs. Sloane's ballroom, Dexter had watched the lady's flight with a wide grin, then made his own farewells and left. This hasty departure, after his last words to Lady Ariel, gave rise in everyone's mind that he was on his way to join her.

He did not intend, however, to see her again this evening, but as he dismissed his carriage and strolled the unlighted streets toward his house, he began to chuckle.

"Yes, my dear," he said aloud, "fly away to safety. But we shall have our accounting – and soon."

NINE

There should certainly be no reason why the sharing of a single dance, even if that dance had been a waltz, and the exchange of a few sentences, most of which she had found incomprehensible, with a gentleman who was so near to being a stranger should disturb her rest. Ariel could not believe this was the cause of her tossing and turning for hours and when she arose the next morning, heavy-eyed, she was more inclined to blame her indisposition upon the unwise action of wearing the soaked petticoat and even managed a sniffle or two to bolster her belief.

Both young ladies descended late to the breakfast table and sat for some time, toying with their food. Ariel was not in the mood for talking, an unusual state for her, and Clarissa was apparently struggling for words.

Finally, she said in an anxious tone, "Ariel, I wish you will not be angry with me for what I have done."

Startled out of her self-absorption, Ariel looked up from the toast which she had been crumbling to bits.

"Angry? Nothing in the world that you could do would make me angry with you, Clare dear."

"But you do not know –" There was another hesitation and Ariel reminded herself that Clare was often overset by things which she considered trifling. Then the words came tumbling.

"James – that is, Mr. MacPherson – brought a message yesterday from his aunt, who has come on a visit to him and his father, asking if I would come to dinner tonight. And I said I would go – without asking what you had planned."

Ariel fought down an impulse to laugh; *this* was the terrible thing her cousin had done? She caught Clarissa's hand and squeezed it.

"Clare dear, you know there is no need for you to ask my permission to go out whenever you wish. Of course I would make an objection if you wished to go with someone who was unsuitable, but I know you too well to think that you would ever do that. Both James and his father are estimable people; I am certain that the aunt will prove to be the same."

"I know that she must be; James has spoken so highly of her. I think he does not remember his mother, and his aunt has

169

done much to take her place. But I ought not to have accepted without asking if you wished me to accompany you."

"If you continue to talk in such a gooseish fashion, I shall – I shall *shake* you," Ariel threatened, only half in jest. "There is no need for you to go anywhere you do not wish to, but I thought that you were enjoying all the balls and parties we have been attending.'

"Oh, I do enjoy them very much, but –" Her words trailed off and Ariel finished for her,

"But you would prefer to be with James." As Clarissa nodded, blushing, her cousin said, "I vow I believe that you have developed a *tendre* for that young man."

"Oh no. He – he has not said anything –"

Ariel jumped up and caught the young girl in her arms.

"You do not have to wait until he speaks to have feelings for him, my sweet goose. Anyway, one has only to take a look at him to tell that he is smitten." She smiled at the radiant look this observation had brought to her cousin's face and went on, "Of course you shall go to dinner with him – and look your best."

"But what about you?"

"Child, I have my choice of half a dozen invitations, and I do not doubt I could find a score of escorts if I wished them. There is no need for you to worry about me."

Clarissa returned the hug, then ran upstairs to decide which gown she should wear and to begin preparations for the evening, for she had no more than seven or eight hours until that important moment when James would arrive. It was true that he had said nothing, but there had been something in his expression when he had tendered the invitation which had made her feel that this might be a *very* important occasion.

Ariel looked after her, smiling. She would have preferred a more illustrious connection for Clare, but it seemed that her heart was set upon James MacPherson. He was a good young man if not a wealthy one, and Clare had no need for wealth when *she* had so much to be shared.

Her smile faded as she considered the invitations she had received for this evening's entertainment. As she had told Clare, she could choose from at least a dozen; but for the first time since she had come to London, she did not feel eager to accept any of them. She told herself that it was only a result of sleeping poorly the night before, but, in truth, it was because she had noticed that several invitations had come from hostesses who were definitely considered by the *ton* to be fast.

She wondered if their preference for her company was an indication that she was getting a similar reputation. Certainly, that had not been her intention. But in her determination to throw to the winds all of the restrictions which Uncle Sylvester had placed upon her life, she feared that she might have gone beyond the line. Those unwelcome attentions she had received from the Regent, from that dreadful Mr. Soames, and, she supposed, from Lord Dexter as well seemed to say that she must have done so.

The gowns she had worn on the last two occasions had certainly been extreme and she knew that they would have been thought unforgivable if it became known that they had been worn by an unmarried girl; but a widow was permitted almost as much freedom as a married woman, so she doubted if any except the highest sticklers would censure her on that account. There were some, she was certain, who would envy the attention she had received from all the beaux – and especially from the Prince Regent.

The malaise persisted, however, and when Clarissa at last presented herself for her cousin's approval, Ariel still had not been able to make a choice among the many invitations.

"What is it? Are you ill?" Clarissa inquired with quick sympathy. It was totally unlike

Ariel not to be eager for the next ball or rout.

"Nothing at all, so do not be concerned. Merely a well-deserved punishment for going out as I did last evening." She sniffed to prove her point and Clarissa, her attention diverted for a moment from the question of Ariel's health, exclaimed,

"Oh, I was so shocked when I saw what you had done," then clapped her hands over her mouth, for she had resolved that she would never again criticize her dearest Ariel, no matter what she might do. If it had not been for Ariel's generosity in bringing her to London, she would never have had a chance to meet James.

The older girl only laughed and admitted, "I was rather shocked, myself, for I could not help thinking of the hands which would have been raised in horror if I had done something of the sort at home. Still, so many of the ladies are doing it that I thought I would see what it is like. It is a most uncomfortable sensation, I can tell you."

"And now you are ill because of it. Ariel, I shall stay at home this evening and care for you."

"You certainly shall not stay, for I am *not* ill. Probably, I shall decide to go out later and shall forget how I feel now. You know that so many of the entertainments here in

London do not begin until after ten of the clock, so there is time to spare. Now, go downstairs and dazzle your young man." She turned Clarissa about and sent her on her way with an affectionate spank.

Clarissa almost ran to the top of the stairs, then made herself pause and take several deep breaths. It would not be at all the thing to seem as impatient to see James as she felt.

In the hall below, he looked up eagerly as she descended the stairs, then caught his breath. Her gown was the same pale blue-green as the sea at sunset, with an overdress of white, sheer except for the tiny flowers embroidered in silver thread at intervals over the skirt. She wore no jewels, but her hair glowed in the candlelight. He thought that she looked more like an angel than she had ever done.

And, like an angel, completely above his touch.

Clarissa noticed at once how his eyes had clouded and came to stand before him, saying anxiously, "You do not like my new gown?"

"It is beautiful," he said with an effort. "And you are beautiful – the most beautiful woman I have ever seen. It is only that I am realizing for the first time how different our worlds must be. I ought not to have brought you my aunt's invitation."

"You mean that this is not the sort of gown I ought to have put on for a dinner party. I suppose that I ought to have known that, but you must remember how ignorant I am about London fashions. It is only that this is my best and I wished for you to see me in it. I can change it at once; I will not make you wait for more than a few minutes."

"No, it is not the gown – although that must be a part of it. It is that you are a lady and I am only a very junior partner in my father's firm."

"No, you are mistaken," she protested. "Ariel is a lady, but I am only her cousin, her very poor cousin. And this gown is a gift from her. You see all of the accounts which come from her dressmakers and know that it is she who pays for everything."

"And it is because I do pay the bills that I know how much gowns such as this one cost. I do not earn enough in half a year to pay for one of them. I realize now that I ought not to have presumed and I shall carry your regrets to my aunt."

"You will do nothing of the kind," Clarissa cried, taking refuge in anger so that she would not burst into tears at his words. She did not know why he should say such things to her; could he know how deeply

175

he was hurting her? "You invited me to go to this dinner and now you *shall* take me."

"But can you not see –"

She stamped her foot.

"I can see perfectly that you are seeking some excuse to go away. If it is truly this gown that you dislike so much, I shall go to Ariel and say, 'Take back all the gowns and all the other gifts you have made to me. Let me have my old gown back that I wore when we came to London. Then perhaps James will not despise me.' "

"Despise you," he cried. "Oh, my dear –"

As he caught her up in his arms, Hodges, who had been waiting to let them out the door, discreetly withdrew from the hall. However, when he later described the scene to Mrs. Hodges, he said, "I doubt if they would have noticed me had I marched past them playing a huge drum." Beneath his pontifical exterior, Hodges concealed a paternal interest in the two young ladies in the house and approved wholeheartedly of the quiet young man Miss Clarissa had chosen.

"You would truly give up all those things for *me?*" James was asking.

"All that and more. I have enjoyed all the fine things, but they would mean nothing without you," a statement which must, of course, be paid for with a great many kisses.

After a number of tender sentiments had been exchanged, James said, "Your guardian –"

"I have not had one since Uncle Sylvester died – unless you should mean Ariel."

"No, I scarcely think she would be considered a proper guardian, because of her age."

He thought it best, knowing how fond his beloved was of her cousin, not to mention how greatly he disapproved of Lady Ariel's behavior. Despite the fact that he did not attend the *ton* parties, stories of her hoydenish activities had come to his ears and he had been afraid that Clarissa might come to prefer such a life as well. How fortunate he was that she had remained the same sweet girl as when she had first come to London.

"My father is much better informed about the law than I; I shall ask him to whom I should speak about our marriage."

"I think you should speak to me," Clarissa declared, thrilled into a boldness she had never possessed by the thought that James loved her and wished her for his wife.

He laughed down at her and said tenderly, "Of course I shall do that, my darling. But since you are not of age, there may be some problems; I do not know, but Father will be able to tell us if there are and how we should move to overcome them."

Much later, he remembered his reason for coming to the house this evening and said, "I fear Aunt will be angry with us for we are going to be very late for dinner, but perhaps she will not be when she learns the reason."

Clarissa would have liked to run upstairs and tell Ariel her wonderful news at once, but she knew that if she did so, it would be a time before she could get away again and it would not be right to keep James' aunt waiting any longer, so she would tell Ariel in the morning.

After she had heard the front door close behind the pair, Ariel decided at last that she would not go out this evening, and sent word downstairs to have a tray brought to her sitting room, saying that she wished nothing except some bread and fruit or perhaps a piece of cheese.

Distressed that he had been given no warning of his mistress' wishes so that he could have concocted one of his special delicacies to please her, the chef nonetheless, remembering her country-bred appetite, sent up a tray piled so high with various foods that Ariel laughed to see it, declaring that it would be impossible for her to eat a quarter of it.

Lord Dexter had spent several fruitless hours looking in upon one or another of the routs and balls being given that evening. He was hoping for another encounter with the "lady," thinking it would be good sport to taunt another time, to see if he could again put her to flight. Without obvious questioning, he had managed to learn that she had not been seen in any of these places and, discounting the fact that he might be ahead of her, he searched out the last place where he would have expected her to be on a busy evening, suspecting that she might be hiding from him.

Her ladyship had made a much larger meal that she had intended and had returned the tray, hoping that her chef would not decide to be insulted because she had not eaten more. She dismissed Parsons for the evening, assuring her that she could prepare herself for bed, for she did not wish to have someone hovering about her. She was wondering if she should descend to the library for a book to help her spend her unaccustomed leisure, and trying to remember where she had left the one she had begun several days ago, when Hodges puffed his way up the stairs to inform her that the Earl of Dexter had called and would like a word with her.

The stiffness in the butler's manner as he delivered this message, added to the fact that he had brought it himself rather than sending it by a footman as was customary, gave proof of his opinion of such a visit.

"At this hour?" As she had told Clare, Ariel had thought that there was something odd in the way his lordship had behaved toward her the evening before, but for him to make a call at an hour when he ought to expect her to be on her way to some ball –

"Please tell Lord Dexter that I have retired," she ordered and saw Hodges' disapproving frown give way to a satisfied nod. That was the way, in his opinion, that presumptuous callers should be treated, whether they were nobles or tradesmen. Years in the service of the Rawls family, especially its present head, had given Hodges no good opinion of the Quality.

Some moments later, he labored his way to her door once more and announced.

"His lordship says that he has no objection to coming up here if your ladyship is abed." The second journey up those long flights of stairs in so short a time had almost been beyond his strength, but he would never have stooped to sending a footman to her ladyship with *that* message. If Lady Ariel said that Lord Dexter might come up, if he had misjudged her character to that extent, he was prepared to give notice on the spot, for his wife as well as for himself.

Fortunately, he was not to be driven to that extreme.

"That is outside of enough!" Ariel cried, shocked to think that even a rake would make so improper a suggestion to a lady he had seen for only two brief meetings.

"Shall I throw Lord Dexter out, my lady?" Hodges asked hopefully, having partially regained his breath.

Despite her anger, the butler's offer made Ariel fight down the impulse to giggle. She was not certain whether it would be proper to expel such an eminent peer as Lord Dexter from her house, no matter how improper *his* behavior might be; and even if it was possible to do so, she could not see her middle-aged and corpulent butler forcibly ejecting the earl, who gave evidence of being very muscular. It would doubtless take the combined efforts of her entire male staff to accomplish such a feat.

However, she appreciated how deep was the old man's concern for her and kept her voice steady as she said, "No, show his lordship into the red saloon and tell him that I shall be down presently. And, Hodges – do not hurry down to give him the message."

Hodges almost smiled at that. When he had begun making his way slowly down the stairs another time, Ariel sat down with her hands folded in her lap, watching the ormolu clock upon the table beside her bed, making certain that a full fifteen minutes had passed before going to her mirror and checking her appearance carefully, repinning several curls which had threatened to fall over her ears and passing the haresfoot lightly over her face. She decided, however, that she would not change her gown. Lord Dexter might call at this hour, but he was not to be made to feel that he was welcome.

As she started down the stairs, she was rehearsing the phrases she might use, determined at first that she would give the arrogant earl the tongue-lashing he deserved for his insulting behavior, then discarding that plan and deciding that icy scorn might be a better way of showing her disapproval. Merely because he had once shown her some little kindness upon the road to London, he need not think he could act as he had done.

Anger flared again as she stepped into the drawing room and looked at her caller. Dexter had poured himself a drink. She could imagine how it had pained Hodges to bring him refreshment but, unless ordered to do so, he would not have neglected his duty had the caller been the devil himself. She felt that the butler considered the present occupant of the room to be a close relative of His Satanic Majesty.

The earl was seated upon a sofa, long legs stretched out before him, sipping from his glass with apparent appreciation. He made no move to rise when she entered, merely fastening his mocking gaze upon her and raising his glass in half-salute.

"You are quite prompt, my dear. When I was told that you had retired, I was certain that it would take you an hour or more – unless you had planned to receive me *en déshabillé*."

Ariel's fingers fairly tingled to slap that mocking look from his face. The man was insolent beyond belief! Yet, even in her anger, she was forced to admit that he was a handsome figure lounging there. His red hair was arranged in the fashion which she had learned was called, "windswept"; it looked careless, but actually took some time to arrange. His evening suit of midnight blue superfine molded itself to what was obviously an athletic figure.

She thought his features might be considered attractive, too, if they had held another expression except for that mocking grin and the disturbing look in his eyes.

That look held the same insolence as his greeting and the message he had sent up to her and she determined that he should be set down at once. In the most cutting tones she could summon up, she asked, "To what do I owe the – honor – of your visit, my lord? This is scarcely the proper hour for a – gentleman – to call upon a lady."

That pose of virtuous indignation was well done, Dexter thought, but certainly she could not have expected that her claiming him as her paramour would not have come to his ears the moment he reached the city and she should know that he would not allow it to pass unchallenged. Still, she was an attractive piece of goods, perhaps not as provocative in her soft green cambric as in the vivid and revealing gown she had worn last evening, but more than passably pretty. He was determined to continue the game at least for tonight before he denounced her.

"I do not think that anyone would consider my being here at this hour so strange," he said in the same lazy tone that Ariel remembered from the night at the posting inn. "Far otherwise, in fact. And under the circumstances, my sweet, do you not think you might bring yourself to call me Randall?"

Was the man mad or merely the worse for drink? As far as she could tell, he did not appear to be foxed, but she had not had much experience with those who were, so could not be certain. She had been told that he was a great rake and certainly his behavior was improper enough to prove that to be true, but did not even rakes wait for some sign of encouragement from the lady they had marked for their attention? After her experiences of several evenings past, she doubted that they did so, but at least, *this* one would receive no encouragement from her.

"I know of no circumstances which would make such familiarity permissible," she said coldly, "nor of any which would excuse the message you sent upstairs by my butler. Neither, my lord, have I given you permission to sit about my house as if it belonged to you, nor to address endearments to me."

"Have you not?" He appeared to consider the question with a great deal of interest. "I should have thought that you would expect both my presence and my endearments. After all, it was not I who led the *ton* – from the Regent down – to think that we are lovers."

"Lord Dexter!"

The indignation in her tone made him chuckle; there was no doubt that she was able to play her part to perfection. Still, he warned,

"Do not attempt to play the innocent with me, my girl. It will not fadge. You cannot be ignorant of what everyone is saying, for it was you who let fall the 'secret' about the two of us. I have that upon the best of authority."

He *must* be mad, she thought, and wondered if he would turn violent and if she should summon Hodges and the footmen to eject him. Glancing in the direction of the bellrope and hoping that she could reach it without arousing his suspicions, she said,

"But – but I did not –" Might it be dangerous to disagree with him?

"Oh, I do not mind," he said lightly. "Although, to be truthful, I was angered when I first heard the stories. Not after I saw you, however. And as long as we have the name –"

Disturbing as both his words and tone might be, they gave no hint of his intentions and her sense of shock at what she considered his derangement was so great that Ariel did not notice when he placed his glass upon the table beside her sofa and reached out a hand toward her. As his fingers closed about her wrist, she tried to pull away, but Dexter drew her swiftly down upon his lap, his arms were tight about her and, before she could voice a protest, his lips were upon hers.

Such behavior as this was the last thing she had expected from him, and Ariel was taken completely off guard. Then the wonder of his kiss held her motionless for a time, her senses whirling. Never had she dreamed a kiss could be like this; the sensation which ran from her lips thoughout her entire being rendered her helpless for some moments.

After a time, however, she began to struggle against him. Even if he was mad, that gave him no right to behave in such a manner toward her. As he raised his head, she drew back her hand to deliver such a blow as had defeated Peter Soames, only to have her wrist caught in a grip so painful that she cried out.

Dexter's eyes were glowing as she imagined those of a wild beast might do as he prepared to make a kill, a look which thoroughly frightened her.

"You little fraud," he said accusingly.

TEN

As she had suspected that his kiss was either the prelude to an improper suggestion or to some other behavior brought on by his obvious derangement, Ariel was so startled by this comment that she could only stare at him for several moments before regaining her breath to ask, "Wah-what do you mean?"

"A complete fraud. Even when I saw you as you appeared last evening, I ought to have realized – that if you were widowed by Waterloo –"

"Talavera." Whatever his reason, he was not to be allowed to trick her into varying her story. She had practiced it too long to make any mistakes now.

"That is even worse. In any case, you would have had to be married from the schoolroom, if not from the nursery – and I cannot see that being done in these times. I am surprised that this has not occurred to anyone else; it is a part with the rest of your lies – you have not taken the trouble to see that your facts fit. Now I am certain that, unless you were still in leading strings and your bridegroom went directly from the ceremony to the battlefield, there never was a wedding. You have never even been kissed until now."

How dare he say that she was a liar? "That is not –"

In the midst of her protest, she recalled that she was still seated upon his knees and she attempted to rise, but he drew her back, holding her tightly against his chest. It was becoming difficult for Ariel to get her breath, less from the force of his arms about her than from the very fact of his nearness.

Drawing a deep breath, she said somewhat defiantly, "I suppose that you are saying that you would know the difference?"

"Certainly I can tell." There was laughter in his tone and she asked, "How?"

Dexter's long fingers imprisoned her chin and turned her face toward his. Ariel thought that he intended to kiss her again and found herself wishing, as dreadfully unladylike as such a thought must be, that he would do so. His kiss had seemed to start tiny fires all through her body and she wondered what had been so different in the way it had held her spellbound than the manner in which a more – experienced – woman would have been affected.

If he kissed her again, she might discover the answer. But he only traced the outline of her mouth with one finger, sending a shiver through her.

"It is true, is it not?" he persisted. "The whole tale of your being a widow with a lover on the string is merely that, a lie. You have never been married."

She wanted to tell him that he was wrong – that she *was* a widow – but the stern look in his eyes made her say, "Yes – I mean, no, I have not been."

His fingers gripped her shoulders with bruising force and he shook her, saying angrily, "Instead of holding you on my knees, I ought to take you across them and lambast you properly, although I suppose it is far too late to beat any sense into you. You little fool – you surely must know that you will be ruined if the truth gets out. It is bad enough now. The ladies of the *ton* are raising their eyebrows at the behavior you have been displaying. As long as they think that you are a widow, however, they might excuse your actions – to a point. An unmarried girl would be cast out entirely for what you have been doing, and you should know it. Whatever made you attempt such a hair-brained scheme?"

"Exactly that," she cried, indignant that he should dare to criticize her after his own behavior of this evening, for she was certain that he had been planning to seduce her.

"Exactly what? That says nothing."

"Having been caged up in the country all of my life, I wished to come to London. But if I came as an unmarried girl, I should have been in no better case here, with a chaperon forever telling me I must not do this or that. A man could never know how confining it would be. It was the only thing I could do – just pretend that I was a widow. And no one knows that I am not, except you – and James."

"Who is James?" Dexter demanded, wondering if there was truly a lover in the offing. If so, he must indeed be a hesitant one, for the earl was certain now that the girl was innocent.

"James MacPherson; he handles my affairs."

"Your what? Oh, your *business* affairs." He laughed in a manner which made her wish to slap him. "For a moment I wondered."

"You have a vile mind," Ariel accused, blushing and making another attempt to rise. He allowed her to leave his knees, but drew her to the sofa beside him, holding her there.

"Perhaps I have," he admitted. "But no worse than the rest of the *ton*, all of whom taken the greatest pleasure in discussing one another's crim. cons."

"Their what?" Ariel had never heard that particular term.

"Their – *affaires*. And it has been your behavior, my girl, which has caused everyone to think of you as they do. But tell me, how did it happen that you chose to use my name?"

"But I did not."

"You must have done. Prinny told me – no, I must admit that he said you had refused to mention any name, but added that the word had got about just the same. So you surely

191

must have said something to give people such an idea."

"I tell you I did not," she said indignantly. "I have never mentioned your name but one time. That was when I told Mr. Baine that you had been kind to me, and he found that difficult to believe, which does not surprise me if you behave as odiously to everyone as you have done here this evening."

"I can assure you," Dexter said, "That I have never behaved with any gentleman of my acquaintance as I have with you – and with only some of the ladies."

He saw her hand double into a fist and placed his own over it so that she could not raise it as he went on, "And what do you mean – kind to you? My dear child, I had never laid eyes upon you until last evening."

"But you did so – it was some weeks ago, at a posting inn on the Bath road. Although I am not surprised that you do not remember. You scarcely glanced at us, so we could not have made the same impression upon you as you did upon me. You told the landlord to let my cousin and me have a room, and even gave us yours, telling the man that we must be virtuous because no drab would allow herself to be seen in such awful gowns as we were wearing."

"You mean *that* was you? That –"

"That dowd who looked as if she had robbed a dustbin for her clothing. I quote your words exactly, my lord."

"If I said such a thing as that, I must beg your pardon. I may have been a trifle foxed at the time, for the landlord stocked some unusually fine brandy for such a place, as I recall."

He had not been too foxed to think that she was a "pretty piece," despite her odd costume, Ariel thought, but resisted the impulse to tell him so. Instead, she reassured him, "I am quite certain that you did not intend us to overhear what you said. And how could you have thought other than what you did of us? But those were the only gowns we possessed."

He looked at her doubtfully, having a dim recollection of the poorly dressed creature she had mentioned and comparing her with the beautifully groomed woman at his side. At least, she had been beautifully groomed before she had struggled to free herself from his embrace; now some of her curls were falling about her ears and her gown had slipped down from her shoulders and was threatening to slip even farther in a most revealing manner.

Seeing his eyes upon her, Ariel reddened furiously and tugged the gown into place.

Then, realizing that the earl already knew that she was not the widow she pretended to be, she began telling him of her early life, of how Sylvester's nip-farthing ways had prevented them from having anything they wished, and of her discovery that she was an heiress and her decision to come to London.

"That was when I decided to call myself a widow, so that I would not be so confined here as I had always been at home," she explained. "And no one but you saw anything wrong with my story. But I had not thought what some people might do."

She went on to tell him of the Prince Regent's attempts to make her the object of his gallantry and of the even more unwelcome attentions of Peter Soames.

"When I attempted to avoid the Regent, he asked me if there was someone else in my life and I thought he would be less angry with me if he were to believe that there was. And I was right; he was most polite after that and took me directly back to the ballroom. I did *not* mention your name to him, however, nor to anyone – I had never even thought of you until Mr. Baine asked if I had ever met a member of the *ton* before coming to London. I did not think that Mr. Soames would be deterred by the talk of an imaginary person as the Regent had been, so –" She remembered a bit of boxing cant she had once heard from Henry and finished, "So I drew his cork."

Dexter threw back his head and laughed heartily.

"That was good enough for him. The fellow's a loose fish – should never be allowed in society, despite his connections. I only wish that I had been there to see you deal with him, but, of course, if I had been, he would have attempted nothing. He is brave only with women or children – if one can call his despicable acts bravery."

Ariel shuddered. "I thought him terrible."

"He is. But enough of him. I suppose that Freddie Baine must have fastened upon your story of my kindness – quite exaggerated, by the way; I am never kind – to decide that I was the man, although how he learned what you had told Prinny, I cannot understand. However, now that I know your terrible secret, I shall keep it – for a price."

Ariel glared at him. What sort of price could he mean? If he was intending to suggest that she should make the stories true by actually becoming his mistress, she would – she did not know what she would do, but it would be something unpleasant. Certainly, he deserved it.

Almost as if he had read her mind, Dexter chuckled.

"You need not overset yourself, my dear. Green girls are not the ones to appeal to me, and I certainly have no wish to marry one."

"M-marry?" That was definitely the last thing she expected that he would have in mind. She did not think him the type to offer to restore her reputation by such chivalrous means.

He laughed again. "Oh, I was not referring to you, then, my love; I would not think you would expect an offer in form and I am not the sort to make one. It is Myrtle Soames. I fear that her redoubtable mama has decided that I would make an ideal husband for her daughter."

"Myrt –" The thought of fat, spotty faced Myrtle Soames and this handsome rake beside her was too much for Ariel. She went off into a fit of giggles and Dexter looked at her sourly.

"You may laugh. But I see nothing comical about it. I am certain that her ladyship intends to try to contrive some situation so that I shall find it impossible to avoid offering for the chit. I believe that you can help me."

"I?"

"Yes – you have merely to allow everyone to go on believing what they already believe about us. It would do neither of us any good to deny it, anyhow. No one ever puts credence in such denials. However, if I should begin to partner you at balls or drive through the Park with you beside me, they will only be convinced that we are becoming less discreet than before about our liaison – which I definitely feel would be enough to put Lady Soames off. I know that she has already heard enough to make her angry at me."

"But why should people – if they already think –" The mere idea of what they *did* think about her and the earl brought a blush to Ariel's cheeks.

He nodded sympathetically, wondering how such an innocent little widgeon as she could have got herself into a coil like this, but realizing that there was no way for her to escape unless she went home to the country. If she remained here, people would continue to talk about her, no matter what she did.

"Oh, they do think that, I assure you. But this will be different. Mind you, I am certain that it would not matter to Lady Soames how badly we behaved, as long as we did not publicize the fact, but if it seems that we are now flaunting our association, she would not be able to ignore it and would doubtless soon come to disapprove of me as a husband for her daughter."

"Oh well –" Ariel said, greatly relieved by the thought that he only wished to dance with her or to take her driving. After all, no one could despise so handsome and important an escort. "If that is all, I have no doubt we can manage to give that impression."

She had no way of knowing that it had been Myrtle Soames who was responsible for the beginning of the rumor about her, but the girl had always behaved hatefully to her and she could not believe that it was only because of the peacock-colored gown. Lady Soames had been even more disagreeable than her daughter and Ariel felt no compunction about doing either of them a disservice. After all, what right had a mere baroness and her daughter to snub the daughter of an earl? Then too, Myrtle was the niece of that detestable Peter Soames.

"If you wish me to be seen with you, I do not mind."

"There may be a little more to it than our merely being seen in company," Dexter said. "I have no doubt there will be times when I am forced to do this."

He caught her hand, turning it palm upward and pressing a kiss upon her wrist. Ariel wondered if he could feel how her pulse had leaped beneath the caress.

He then brushed back a strand of hair which had been disarranged and she could feel his lips tracing the outline of her ear.

Nearly suffocating, Ariel closed her eyes, wondering what liberty he would attempt next, and if it would be within her power to prevent it, for his very touch seemed to melt her bones.

Dexter's chuckle made her eyes fly open to meet his mocking gaze.

"Nothing more," he said, as if he had once more read her mind. "There will be nothing which may not be done before others, although we shall make it appear that we think ourselves unobserved. I only wished you to be prepared for such caresses as we might be forced to be seen exchanging from time to time. We shall make it appear that we are endeavouring to be discreet, but are sometimes overcome by our feelings for one another. And there is something else. I think that your servants had best be prepared to have me call here at unconventional hours. Servants are quite as prone to gossip as members of the *ton* and we must give them a reason to gossip."

Ariel chuckled in her turn and when he looked at her, eyebrows raised, explained,

"I was only thinking of how shocked Hodges – and Mrs. Hodges, as well – will be at being given such orders. I hope that they will not decide they can no longer remain in my service because of this new – indiscretion.

I think you should know, my lord, that when you called this evening, Hodges requested my permission to throw you out of the house."

Dexter's head went up haughtily at the thought of such presumption on the part of a servant, then the memory of the butler's age and his rotund form made him see the humor in the situation and his laughter joined her own.

"That is loyalty indeed, but I am surprised that you did not permit him to try it, my love."

Ariel blinked at the endearment, then reminded herself that it was only a part of their charade and meant no more to him – and to her, of course – than having his arm stretched across the back of the sofa, his fingers toying with the ruffle of soft lace which edged the neck of her now decorously arranged gown.

She leaned forward, afraid of her own feelings if his fingers should chance to touch her throat. It was easy enough to see why the man was so successful a rake, for he had the power to stir up emotions she had not known that she possessed. A girl less level-headed than she might easily have her defenses swept away by those endearments, by the touch of those practiced fingers and lips.

In as light a tone as she could manage, she

retorted, "I must confess that I was strongly tempted to do so, especially after the insulting message you sent up."

"For which I now offer my apologies. It was sent in ignorance of the true situation."

She nodded acceptance. "But I had gathered the impression that you might not submit tamely to being thrown. And although Hodges is not a family retainer – at least, not of *my* family – I should not wish to see him harmed."

"So all of your concern was for Hodges. You gave no thought to my well-being."

"Not in the slightest, my lord."

He laughed appreciatively. "Very good indeed. I think our association may well prove to be an enjoyable one, even if it is not precisely the one I had planned."

Ariel felt herself blushing once more, and thinking that in all of her life, no one had ever been able to put her to the blush as this outrageous man could do. Watching her, Dexter grinned wickedly. He had noticed how she had drawn away from his touch and was certain that it was not dislike of him which had caused the withdrawal. However, he was wise enough in the ways of women not to comment upon it.

Instead, he was thinking of some remarks which would tease her further without going too far beyond the line, but was interrupted by a tap at the door. Hodges put in his head to ask, "Would your ladyship like to have the tea tray brought in now, as usual?"

"Y-yes, Hodges," Ariel managed to say, although there was nothing usual about their having tea in the evening. Dexter had noticed her hesitation and commented with a laugh as Hodges withdrew,

"Since you refused to allow him to throw me out, it seems that your estimable butler plans to hint me away, knowing that the proper visitor will feel obliged to take his leave after tea has been served. But I warn you that he will not be successful; he will have to learn that I am *not* a proper visitor."

"I – I think he may already have gathered that fact," Ariel told him with a smile.

Still, she was happy that he rose and went to lean against the mantel as the tea tray was brought in under Hodges' supervision, for she had felt the old man's disapproval when he had noted Dexter's familiarity. He might well have had a spasm, she thought, had he come into the room while she was being held on his lordship's lap.

"Perhaps you would prefer something other than tea?" she suggested, but Dexter said,

"No, at this hour, I think tea would be enjoyable."

He came to her side to take the cup she had filled, then retired to a more respectful distance as if this were an ordinary occasion. Taking a few sips of tea, he picked up several books which were lying upon the table and began talking about them.

"Yes," Ariel said, "I found these in the library and brought them in here, hoping for a chance to read them, but have not had time to read more than a page or two since I came to London. You would have thought that I would have had enough of reading at home, where, when our tasks were done, there was nothing for us to do except to read. It is not true, however; I still enjoy my books."

"But surely not such books as these – histories and books of travel. I thought ladies only cared for Mrs. Radcliffe's novels or the poems of Lord Byron."

"You have learned my guilty secret; I enjoy reading books which have some substance to them. I fear the blame for my tastes must be laid at my father's door."

"In what way? From what you have told me, he would scarcely have had the time to train you into such habits of reading."

"He did not, for I scarcely remember him. But he had a great many books and his favorite ones were so badly worn that they were not worth the selling, so Uncle Sylvester permitted me to keep them, on the condition that I did not neglect my work to read. Later, he decided that they would make good fuel."

"You mean that he actually burned books?" Dexter was shocked, but she said matter-of-factly,

"Why not? They were at hand and it was cheaper than buying fuel. But I managed to hide a number of them. My taste was formed by those books. If I had known that I was to have a visitor, however, I should certainly have put them out of sight, for I have learned since coming to London that nothing is worse for a female than to be thought bookish. I can only hope that I can depend upon you not to reveal it."

"Yes, that would certainly be worse than anything else they might say about you," Dexter agreed, picking up one of the books again and leafing through it.

He had read it, but she had not yet had a chance to do so, so they began by speaking of it, then went on to other books. They talked for more than an hour and Ariel was surprised to find that Dexter was more widely read than she. She had learned that many gentlemen were as fearful of being thought bookish as were their female companions. As for the earl, she would have supposed that his – activities – would have left him little time for reading.

However, she said nothing of these thoughts, for she had discovered that talking to him was quite pleasant and she wished to do nothing to spoil the mood. They had found that they had many of the same favorites and were hardly aware of Hodges' extreme disapprobation when he entered with the footman to remove the tea tray and learnt that his lordship, instead of preparing to take his leave, was deep in earnest conversation with Lady Ariel.

He complained to Mrs. Hodges about her ladyship's lack of discretion in making friends with such a rake and found that, for once, she was not in agreement with him. Beneath her solemn exterior, Mrs. Hodges was a romantic and could understand why Ariel should be fascinated by the earl.

"The trouble with you, Hodges, is that you are not a female," she said, goading him into saying sharply, "I thank the Lord I am not, for I would be ashamed to act so foolish."

At last, Dexter rose reluctantly to make his *adieux*, aware that he had actually enjoyed the evening – the most unusual of any he could remember having spent with a lady. Lady Ariel was actually a charming little thing beneath her pretence of worldly wisdom. Yet he could sense that there was a love of mischief in her and he believed that she was looking forward as eagerly as he to the rig they were going to run upon the members of the *ton*, and especially upon such matchmaking mamas as Lady Soames.

"Shall I see you at Devonshire House tomorrow night?" he asked.

"Yes, we have been invited." The situation at Devonshire House had long been such an irregular one that no one who went there would be surprised at the widow's presence.

"We?" His eyebrows went up as he wondered with whom the lady was planning to attend the ball and was prepared to warn her that he would be expected to take objection to her favoring anyone other than himself.

"My cousin Clarissa – you certainly would not remember her any more than you remembered me, but we were together at the posting house."

He nodded, having a vague recollection that there had been two of the young females, but the fair-haired one had made even less of an impression upon him than her darker companion, so he had supposed that if *she* had been Lady Ariel, the other must have been her abigail. Yet he believed that she had said something earlier in the evening about having been accompanied by her cousin.

"And does your cousin often leave you to entertain visitors alone?" If she did so, and especially if the visitors were gentlemen, that was another reason for gossip about her behavior.

"Not often, but she had an invitation for this evening which did not include me. But you need not worry; I shall explain our situation to her and I am certain she will understand."

She was far less certain of that than she sounded. Clare would doubtless be shocked at the arrangement, but she must be brought to see that there was really nothing else that her cousin could do, since people were gossiping about her in that dreadful way. In fact, Dexter had been right when he guessed that Ariel was beginning to look forward to their charade.

Something far different occurred to her now and she asked, "May I persuade you to do something for me, my Lord?"

"Randall."

"Even when we are alone?"

"Especially when we are alone, my dear. You must become so accustomed to saying it that you will never call me by any other name. You could say, 'Dexter,' as most people do – but you might slip and call me, 'Lord Dexter' – and you can see that would be fatal to our scheme. Then, too, if you say 'Randall,' it will sound more intimate."

Ariel's eyes danced. "And what if I should say, 'Randal – oh, I ought to have said Lord Dexter'? Would that not give them even more to gossip about?"

"Good girl," he said in so approving a tone that she felt he might pat her on the head as if she were a child or an obedient puppy. "That is exactly the impression we mean to convey."

"Then, Randall I ought to say Lord Dexter – will you do something for me?"

"If it is not out of reason, certainly."

"Will you make it clear to Mr. Soames that he – that is, that I am not –"

"Not available?" he asked, his mocking tone bringing a flush to Ariel's cheeks, but she said in a low voice,

"Something of the sort. I would not wish to have any more trouble with him."

"I do not think it likely that you will do so, after having treated him so cruelly, especially now that he believes that you are mine. But I shall speak to him, nonethless; it will be a good excuse to give him the sort of setdown he needs. He should never have been allowed to come near you."

"Tha-thank you." Why should the mere fact that he was willing to do this for her make her suddenly feel so – protected? She told herself sternly that this was only because she was relieved that Mr. Soames would no longer trouble her.

"I do not believe, however," Dexter said with a grin, "that it will be necessary for me to give a warning of the same sort to Prinny. He is already beside himself with fear of what I might do to him for his indiscreet actions toward you."

Ariel could not help laughing at the thought.

"Oh, the poor old man." She clapped her hands over her mouth. "Oh, I should not have said that."

"*Lèse majesté*, certainly. But I shall not give you away."

"But – but I did not know what to do. Think how terrible it would have been if I had slapped him."

"He probably would have burst into tears and rushed off to Lady Coyningham for comfort, and doubtless would have received a severe scold for his misbehavior."

Dexter joined in her laughter at the picture he had conjured. Then he sobered and took her hands in his.

"Perhaps it was wrong of me to make such a suggestion to you. Your reputation will be quite ruined if we go on with it."

Uncomfortably aware of his nearness, of the feeling which ran though her at the touch of his hands, Ariel knew only that she must go ahead with this because he wished it, so endeavoured to speak lightly.

"I fear that it must already be in tatters, if they have been speaking of me as you say. They will not stop doing so, will they, even if we do nothing."

Throwing back her head, she went on defiantly, "Considering what I have seen of London these past weeks, it will take much to shock anyone. If we can succeed in doing so, so much the better."

Dexter bowed low and brought her hand to his lips, aware of how her fingers trembled in his grasp.

"I salute your daring, my dear – and between us, we shall succeed in hoaxing them right royally."

ELEVEN

After Dexter had gone, shown out by Hodges – who had made no secret of the fact that he considered it most improper of the earl to have called alone upon her ladyship at such an hour and to have remained closeted with her for so long – Ariel had retired, but not to sleep. Unlike the night before, however, she could not blame her wakefulness upon anything other than the feelings which had been stirred up by the presence of that red-haired gentleman.

What had made her consent to so mad a scheme, she asked herself over and over. Had it been merely because his lordship had blackmailed her into agreeing by his threat to expose her? Would he really have done so if she had refused?

Remembering the bold look in his amber eyes, she thought that he would be capable of doing anything.

Still, *had* she agreed out of fear that he would expose her to the *ton* as an unmarried girl who had disgraced herself by racketing about London in so abandoned a fashion, or was it rather that there was something about the man which made it impossible for her to do anything other than what he wished?

"He did give me a chance to withdraw," she said aloud. "I might have done so, but I did not. So he is not entirely to blame. Besides, I think it may be exciting to hoax all those people another time."

In the darkness, she put her fingers to her lips, remembering how his kiss had burned through every fiber of her being; a kiss which, she was certain, had meant nothing more to him than a prelude to further lovemaking, until he had discovered that she had never been kissed before. That discovery had appeared to anger him, although she thought he was also amused at learning that she was so inexperienced.

How could he have known that? What was there about the way she had received his kiss to tell him that it was her first? If he had kissed her again, as she had thought he might do, would she have learned what she ought to have done?

Although there had been no one at home to tell her such things, she had learned since coming to London that a proper young female was expected to feel that she had been insulted if a gentleman tried to kiss her. But from the way some of the girls discussed such matters, it did not seem that many of them actually felt that way. Certainly, she had not done so, and Lord Dexter's intentions had been as insulting as any gentleman's could be.

She pressed a kiss against her palm, but the sensation was not there. Apparently it took a man's lips to stir that feeling inside her, and yet she was positive that if Peter Soames had succeeded in kissing her, she would not have felt this way. The very thought of having him touch her, of feeling his lips upon hers, filled her with disgust. And yet, was he any more of a rake than Dexter?

She did not think that she would have enjoyed it if the Regent had kissed her, either; she did not know why she should believe that, but she did so. It would seem that the only one who could stir her in this fashion was that red-haired rake of an earl.

"Randall," she whispered. "I must never forget to call him Randall," and finally fell asleep, wondering if she truly could be as shameless as everyone thought her, for she was sorry that he had not kissed her a second time.

It was late when she awoke, to find Clarissa seated upon the edge of the bed, looking down at her with shining eyes.

"Oh, I could hardly wait for you to waken," the younger girl cried, "for the most wonderful thing has happened. I nearly stopped to tell you last night, but I made certain that you could not yet have come home from whatever ball you had attended."

Ariel had heard the footsteps as Clarissa passed her door, but she was too confused by her own emotions to wish to exchange confidences. Now she said, "No, I decided that I should retire early last evening, for I thought I was beginning to look a bit haggard with so much trotting. But tell me, what is so wonderful?"

"James wishes to marry me. Oh Ariel, I am the happiest girl in all the world."

Ariel pushed herself up in bed and caught her cousin's hands.

"That is truly what you wish?"

"Yes – yes – from the first moment I saw him, I believe. He is so kind, so thoughtful, so –" Overwhelmed by the thought of the countless virtues James possessed, she flung her arms about Ariel and burst into tears.

The other girl patted her soothingly. "If he is so wonderful as that, and I do not doubt that he is, there is no need for tears. Far from it, I should think. And you know I wish you happy with him, my dear. But are you certain that you would not prefer someone richer, more important – one of the gentlemen who have been giving you so much attention?"

"Oh no, none of them could be nearly so fine as my James." There was pride in the way she spoke those last words. "He may not have a title and he will never have a great deal of money, but he is better than all of the others. Wait until you fall in love, Ariel; then you will understand what I mean. I have enjoyed attending all of the balls and entertainments for a time, but I do not care as much for them as you do. I would truly prefer a quieter life – the sort I will have when I am married to James."

"And have you made all your plans?" It occurred to Ariel that it would be a wrench to give up her constant companion of the past eight years, but Clare must not be allowed to suspect that, for she would feel guilty about leaving.

"No. James has spoken to his father and Mr. MacPherson is going to learn if there will be any problems because I am under age and do not have a guardian except for you, and you are not of age yet, so could not give your consent."

"I do give it – most heartily, dear."

"I know that you do, and it is your consent I wish more than any other. But there may be some legal matter; Mr. MacPherson thinks that there might be, but he has never dealt with a situation exactly like this, so he wishes to look into it. He has no doubt it can be solved. He is so kind – just like James. He has already told me that I must call him Father. It will be so nice to have a father again."

"I know." Ariel's thoughts went to her own dimly remembered father and the cousins held each other tightly for a moment. Then Clarissa went on,

"I love James' aunt as well. Oh, I shall

be so happy – except for missing you. But perhaps you could come and live with us. That would be perfect. I shall ask James if you may do so; I am certain that he would like it as much as I."

"And I am certain that he would not," Ariel told her, laughing.

James had been careful to give no inkling of his disapproval of her way of life. His natural courtesy would have made him slow to offer any criticism of a lady; also, he would not wish to insult so valuable a client. Still, Ariel had been aware from time to time of a slight restraint in his manner toward her, and she was aware that, even if this had not been the case, the last thing a newly married man would wish would be a third person in his home.

"James will wish you all to himself," she assured her cousin. "And you will find that you feel the same. There is no reason why we should not visit each other often. But it would not do for me to live with you and especially not at this time." How fortunate it was that Dexter's – Randall's – plan had come at this time; it would help take her thoughts away from the parting with Clare.

"Why not now?"

"Because – oh, my dear, I fear that you will be shocked when I tell you – but it is not what it will seem. You see, Lord

Dexter called here last evening."

"Lord Dexter? Here? You mean –"

"Yes, the gentleman we met at the posting inn on the road to London. He was at Mrs. Sloane's party and I danced with him. You will remember that I told you about it."

"Yes, but I do not understand. You have danced with many gentlemen, and they do not come calling late at night."

"Many of them would do so, you may be certain, if I allowed them to do so."

"But why have you permitted Lord Dexter to call? And especially when you were alone? You know what he is – what people will say if they hear of it. And what do you mean – that it is not what it will seem?"

Ariel laughed at the thought that she had "permitted" Dexter to call. Her laugh also hid some nervousness. If it was proving to be an embarrassment just to tell Clare, who loved and trusted her, what she was about, how could she ever manage to carry off such a charade before others, many of whom were already critical of her? Of course, that was the difference. These people already believed her to be *fast*, and Clare knew that she was not. She hoped that Clare would not hear the rumors about her which Dexter said were diverting the *ton*.

"I did not permit him to call precisely.
217

Certainly, you must not think that I had invited him. But he did call and suggested that – well, to tell you with no roundaboutation – his lordship and I shall pretend to be interested in one another."

"What?" Clarissa shrieked the word, almost tumbling off the side of the bed in her surprise. "Ariel, you cannot be serious about this. The man is a – a rake. You must remember what James told us about him. You must have nothing to do with him."

Remembering how his lordship had declared, "Green girls have never appealed to me," Ariel said, "You need not worry, Clare. I shall be in no danger from Lord Dexter; I am certain of that. And, whatever his reputation, he is received everywhere. As a matter of fact, his – friendship – may protect me from the unwanted attentions of some other gentlemen."

"But how can you be certain what such a man might say or do? I know you think yourself awake on every suit, as James would say, but you are not, truly. And think of your reputation if you are seen about with him."

"My reputation can be no worse than it is now," Ariel said bitterly, then, noting how that remark had shocked her cousin, hastened to say, "What I mean is that no one will think any the worse of me for being seen with him.

As I said, he is welcomed everywhere, – and you know that a widow may do these things."

Thank Heavens, she thought, that Clare did not suspect what the *ton* was already saying about her and Dexter. But if they thought *that* – and she did not doubt that Dexter was telling the truth – the actions of the Regent and Peter Soames, and the warm remarks of the other gentlemen were even more difficult to understand. Still, her conversation with Mr. Baine had not come until after those encounters. The more she thought of it, the more confusing the entire situation became.

"But you are not a widow," Clarissa was protesting, as she had done in the past, and again Ariel said,

"Aside from the two of us, almost no one knows that."

One of the few who did know the truth about her was, of course, Lord Dexter, and it was this knowledge which made Ariel safe from him. He considered her a green girl, and they did not appeal to him. "And," she went on, "I can tell you, Clare, that no one will think it odd if he escorts me to balls or takes me riding."

"Well, you ought to have an escort," Clarissa conceded, having just discovered how wonderful it could be to have one

— a devoted one. "But he ought to be a gentleman."

"Lord Dexter is a gentleman by title, if not by reputation."

He was much more gentlemanly in his behavior, also, than many of the others had proved themselves to be, Ariel thought. At least, he had not behaved *too* badly after he had learned the truth about her.

Peter Soames, she was certain, would not have withdrawn for an instant if he had discovered her innocence. She believed that he would have been only too happy to have ruined her, and, doubtless, he would have boasted about it later. Dexter might be arrogant, he most certainly was a rake, but he *had* given her an opportunity to withdraw from the agreement. In a like position, would any of the others have done so?

"Let us not argue about the matter, Clare," she coaxed. "For I intend to allow his lordship to escort me about, at least for a time. Let us talk of something else. Although you and James have not yet made your wedding plans, I do not doubt that you have a number of thoughts of what you would wish to do."

Clarissa was easily diverted to this much more interesting topic, but Ariel was certain that her objections would not be forgotten. However, by the time she returned to them,

Ariel was quite certain that her "relationship" with the rakish earl would be so much a matter of public knowledge that there would no longer be any use in Clare's protesting about it.

It was Lord Dexter who provided the gossips with the ammunition they needed, if any more had been required. The next afternoon, he and several friends were about to enter the doors of White's when Peter Soames came out with some of his cronies. Soames was not a member of the club, but the other gentlemen were. The fact that he had been allowed within doors in any company infuriated the earl.

"A word with you, Soames," he called and the other man stopped, greatly surprised for, as fervently as he had often wished to be admitted to the circle of his lordship's acquaintance, Dexter had never spoken to him before.

There was a pleased smirk upon his face as he turned to ask, "In what way may I serve you, my lord?" The smile faded as Dexter, realizing that he could scarcely forbid the man to enter the club when other members – however misguided – had invited him, said the first words which came into his mind. "Lady Ariel Laurence."

There was a tug at Dexter's arm and his

friend David Mortimer said in an undertone, "Not here, Dex – whatever the reason – not the thing to use a lady's name –"

He was right, of course, but the sight of the other man had roused the earl's ire beyond reason. He shrugged himself free of his friend's hand as he said,

"Yes – here – for I wish to make it clear to this loose screw that he is not to annoy the lady further and I wish everyone to know that he has been warned."

"Who said that she was annoyed?" Soames demanded, smirking once more; he was not above a bit of prevarication if it would further his reputation as a lover. Like others, he had heard the rumors about Dexter and Lady Ariel, but he had given them little credit. If the lady had spurned *his* attention, she would certainly have spurned Dexter's as well. "She may tell *you* that, but –"

His words were cut as Dexter's fist caught him in the mouth, lifting him completely off his feet and sending him hurtling down the steps, almost into the street, causing two wandering dogs to begin barking at him shrilly and a passing jarvey to curse as his poor horse shied away from the falling body.

As Soames struggled to his feet, blood trickling from the corner of his mouth, his friends hurried down to help him, insisting that he should call the earl out for striking him.

"Yes, do that, Soames," Dexter said, his hot fury giving way to a cold anger which made him even more dangerous. "It would give me the greatest pleasure to blow a hole through you."

Mr. Soames took a step forward, then hesitated. The blow had angered and humiliated him and he would have liked to demand satisfaction, but he was aware of the earl's reputation as a crack shot and did not doubt that he could easily do as he had threatened. He turned to walk away, saying in a surly tone,

"The jade's not worth fighting about."

Dexter sprang after him and caught his arm.

"If it comes to my ears, and you may be certain that it will, that you have ever mentioned Lady Ariel's name or referred to her in any manner, I warn you that I shall horsewhip you the length of the Strand and back." He dropped Soames' arm and, taking out his handkerchief, wiped his hand as if the contact had soiled it.

The action was even more insulting than the threat, but as Peter Soames had refused to challenge at the time he had been struck, he thought it better not to do so now. There was nothing for him to do but to continue to walk away, his friends looking at him oddly and wondering if it might not be wiser to cut all connections with one so cowardly.

Watching him go, Mr. Mortimer shook his head and said, "I know that you sneer at conventions, Dex, but that was not at all the thing to have done. The man deserves the blow and the threat, I'll grant you that. But it ought not to have been done in public, at least with a lady's name brought into it."

Dexter shrugged, but secretly he was feeling a bit ashamed of the action. Nothing he could have done would have publicized the *affaire* as quickly as this encounter but, as Mr. Mortimer had said, it was not the right thing to have done by Lady Ariel. Actually, there had been no thought of her in the earl's mind when he accosted Peter Soames, but he should not have used her as an excuse for the quarrel.

Until now, all of the scandal had been brought about her head by the girl herself, simply because she had been too green to realize what she was doing. Now, without that excuse for himself, he had involved himself in a public brawl over her; and if there had been the slightest chance of restoring her reputation, it had vanished.

Mr. Mortimer, of course, was too much of a gentleman to say anything of what had happened, but the other witnesses to the quarrel were less discreet and, within hours, the *ton* was chortling over the fact that the Earl of Dexter had knocked down Peter Soames and had threatened to horsewhip him publicly because of his attentions to Lady Ariel.

When the story reached the Prince Regent, His Highness cancelled all his engagements for the next week and cowered within doors, so that there would be no chance of his encountering the earl until that gentleman's temper had a chance to cool. It was not that he physically feared Dexter, he told himself – remembering, with a shudder, the earl's prowess with his fists, even as he said that – but he did not feel that he could afford the scandal of a public brawl.

As he entered Devonshire House that evening, the earl intercepted a number of shrewd glances exchanged and saw several people nudge one another, a clear indication to him that the story of his attack upon Peter Soames, and the reason for it, had become public knowledge. Again, he felt a touch of shame that he had further smirched Ariel's reputation by his action, but when he saw that two or three of the matchmaking mamas who had previously encouraged their daughters to cast out lures in his direction were now drawing them away from him, he thought that his scheme was beginning to work.

Either Lady Soames had not yet decided that he should be cut or else – which he thought quite probable – her daughter was disobeying her mama's instructions, for Myrtle continued to cast simpering glances in his direction. To what lengths must he go, he wondered, to discourage that muffin-faced chit?

Ariel entered the ballroom with Clarissa beside her and was immediately aware that she was the object of glances and gossip. She had become accustomed to receiving attention but, for the first time, wondered what the people might be saying of her.

Tonight she was gowned in deep sapphire blue, the cloth as sheer as the gown she had worn two evenings before. This time, however, there was no dampened petticoat underneath, but an underdress of silver satin which gleamed through the silk.

"Anyone can see that is all Dexter's doing," ran the tattle from one onlooker to another. "He does not wish her to disport herself before any gentleman other than himself."

Having decided to wear this gown rather than another one under which she might have had a dampened petticoat simply because she had found that fashion to be uncomfortable,

Ariel would have been surprised to know what was being said. Dexter, who had heard the talk, was amused for he had enjoyed watching the lady in her revealing gown.

Still, he realized that, especially after this morning's scene with Peter Soames, he was supposed to be playing the jealous lover so stepped ahead of the other gentlemen and swept her onto the dance floor.

"I fear that, as long as our charade continues, you will have no other partner than myself for these waltzes, my love," he told her softly so that anyone near them would think that he was uttering endearments. "All your flirts will be too frightened to offer to do more than lead you through the country dances."

Very much aware of his arm firmly about her waist, of his holding her so much closer than the prescribed distance – so close, in fact that their bodies almost touched as they moved about the floor – Ariel strove to keep her voice as light as his when she said,

"But when you waltz so well, my l-Randall; why should I wish another partner?"

"Very good," he said approvingly, "except for the near-slip about the name. But seriously, my dear, I must admit that I did you a disservice today. I warned Soames off as I promised I would do, but I ought to have

227

done so privately. Instead, I accosted him in the doorway at White's and, as you inelegantly put it, drew his cork for a remark he made about you."

Startled, she looked up to meet his eyes, which held such a gleam that her own fell into confusion. What a play-actor he would have made, she thought; if she had not been warned of his game, she might have believed that he truly cared for her.

"How brave of you to do battle for me, my" – his hand squeezed hers warningly and she quickly said – "dear."

"Naught of bravery about frightening one so hen-hearted," he said, bringing her to a halt before a group of young gentlemen as the music ceased. "But what is mine, I keep."

Several of the others had started forward, but stopped at his words, which had been uttered for their benefit. Seeing them, Dexter smiled in a manner which she knew was mocking her other admirers and said, "Enjoy yourself with whomever you will, my own, but remember that the next waltz is mine."

TWELVE

The earl moved away as he spoke and, realizing that he was apparently not intending to object to their presence, two or three of the bolder gentlemen sought her hand for the upcoming dances. Determined to show that she could play out the charade as well as he did, Ariel looked to where Dexter was leaning against the wall, arms folded, as if she were asking his permission. When he nodded, she accepted as many of the offers as she could.

She did not mind at all that he planned to keep the waltzes for himself, as he did, indeed, waltz better than almost any other gentleman. If only it was not so disturbing to be held so near him, to see him looking as if he might kiss her there in the middle of the floor. The thought of how such an occurrence would shock the dowagers made her giggle and her partner gave her an affronted look, thinking that she was laughing at his lack of skill.

Lady Jersey, who had, like everyone else, heard the story of the morning's encounter and who had not missed a moment of the earlier play, moved to the earl's side.

"Really, Dexter," she said a bit spitefully, for he had neglected to flirt with her as had always been his custom – an attention which she expected from all gentlemen of her acquaintance – "how did it happen that you allowed your little charmer to come to London alone? Did you not fear she might get into mischief?" As she did, the tone implied.

"Just a simple misunderstanding, Sally," he said hastily. "I had promised to bring her to the city, but was delayed by business on one of my estates. The sweet creature became impatient and thought to teach me a lesson by making her way to London with only her little cousin. I came hotfoot as soon as I learned what she had done."

"And have been behaving much like a jealous bridegroom ever since you arrived. I have heard of your *tracasserie* with Peter Soames – who is a detestable man, to be sure – but to make such a threat! Are you certain you are not about to be buckled?" If it was so, her ladyship wanted to be one of the first to know, for what an *on-dit* that would make – Rake Dexter caught at last.

He gave her a startled glance, for that was a conclusion he had not expected anyone to draw, then broke into a laugh.

"Hardly that, Sally, my dear; hardly that."

"Well, I have heard that she had already prepared your bedroom, so I fear she must be expecting an offer from you. So sad for her if she has mistaken your intentions."

That remark startled him even more than the other, although he managed to give no sign. *Had* the minx actually prepared a bedroom for some lover? Surely he could not be as mistaken as all that about her character.

"You should not jump to conclusions, Sally," he said, hoping that he had not given her any inkling that what she had said was news to him. "The occupant of a bedroom need not necessarily be a husband – *you* should know that."

Instead of being insulted, her ladyship laughed and tapped him with her fan. The fact that Dexter was looking forward to staying in the house Lady Ariel had taken was *almost* as interesting an item as if they had been planning to marry. At least, Dexter had not denied that the room was his, which was as good as an admission to the gossip, although if he had denied it, they would still have believed it to be true.

She hastened away to whisper what she thought she had learned and the earl looked after her, swearing beneath his breath. It seemed that every time he opened his mouth, he drove another nail into the coffin of Ariel's reputation. He should never have suggested this bacon-brained scheme to her.

But what about that bedroom? She would have some explaining to do about *that*, if it existed, he told himself, even while he admitted that he had no right to ask any explanation of her. Still, if she was not so innocent as he had thought, it would make a difference in his behavior to her.

When he claimed Ariel for the next waltz, however, he decided that he would postpone questioning her until they went down to the supper room. At supper they were not completely alone, so he thought such a discussion would be best left until some time when no one else was about.

There was opportunity in plenty during their drives in the Park, but the subject did not arise. The truth was that Dexter prided himself that he had judged the lady correctly and shied off from a discussion which might prove him wrong. In any event, Ariel was spending so much of her time in his company that she could not possibly be entertaining any other gentleman.

Unaware of the question which Dexter was avoiding so carefully and which, had she known what he thought or been given any reason to remember the things which Sir Percy had left in his room, she could have answered to his complete satisfaction, Ariel was beginning to have doubts of her own about the wisdom of continuing this charade.

It was most pleasant to have the escort of a handsome gentleman, to know that all eyes, many of them envious ones, were upon them as he tooled his phaeton through the Park with her at his side or led her about the dance floor. Not that she had lacked for escorts since her arrival in London, any more than she had needed to worry that she might have to sit out a dance or miss getting her fill of compliments.

None had courted her as assiduously as the earl was pretending to do, although there were many who were willing to do so, if she had given them the slightest encouragement, for beautiful heiresses were scarce indeed.

"The trouble," Ariel told herself, "is merely that I know that Randall's attentions are different from the others."

They were different because she knew *he* did not mean them and she could not be certain, whatever she might suspect, about the others. As soon as she had helped him to give Lady Soames and the others a disgust of his behavior, this would end. She could only hope that he would permit the *affaire* to come to a finish gradually, as if by mutual consent.

It would be too humiliating if he should cease his attention suddenly.

Humiliating – and disappointing.

"I don't want them to end," she whispered, although she knew that they must. Then, sternly telling herself that she ought not to behave so foolishly, she began to prepare for another ball.

For the past several years, Lady Jersey had given parties only rarely, preferring to be a guest so that she would have more freedom to make her way from one group to another, gathering bits of the scandal she loved. Her friends were surprised, therefore, to receive invitations to her ball, but her ladyship felt that she had been driven to this. Surely, once they were beneath her own roof, she could learn more about the affair which had everyone gossiping.

Certainly, Dexter had never before behaved with any lady as he was doing with Lady Ariel. He had always had his flirts, but his liaisons with ladies of quality had been handled with more discretion. Where had he met Lady Ariel? How had she enticed him to the point that he danced attendance only upon her, ignoring all the other hopefuls? So far, no one had learned the answers, but Sally Jersey was determined that she would discover them if anyone was able to do so.

"I am counting upon you to bring Lady Ariel, Dexter," she said and her archness was rewarded with one of his mocking smiles as he said, "You may depend upon it, Sally; I shall do so – but how kind of you to remind me of it."

Lady Jersey pouted, but was all the more determined to learn the truth of the affair.

Clarissa had not been included in the invitation and Ariel was ready to send her regrets until the younger girl told her, "No, truly I do not mind, for Mrs. MacPherson – James' aunt – has invited me to attend a lecture with her that evening."

"Oh, that is nice," Ariel said, wondering how her cousin could prefer a lecture to a ball, and one given by Lady Jersey at that. A bit guiltily, she added, "I have been neglecting you these past days, have I not?"

"I do not think so." Clarissa spoke as if in a half daze. "I have been so much with James that I have not noticed."

"That is nice," Ariel said again, weakly this time. It had not occurred to her that the time would come when Clare would not know whether or not she was about. For several moments she wondered what her life would be like after her cousin was married, but she resolutely put that thought aside and began thinking of tonight's ball instead.

Dexter looked at her approvingly when Hodges, whose unfavorable opinion of his lordship had not lessened in the slightest despite her ladyship's obvious interest in him, ushered him into the drawing room where Ariel was waiting. Her gown was of deep green, embroidered with gold thread in a design of flowers, each petal glistening with a crystal dewdrop.

"You are perfect, my love, as always," he told her, bowing deeply over her hand. Ariel broke into a laugh when she noticed that he also wore green, his satin evening coat and breeches a darker shade than her gown, making his snowy waistcoat and cravat a purer white by comparison.

When he looked at her, eyebrows raised, she explained, "One would think we had planned this," and indicated her gown and his coat.

"That should give them another reason to gossip about us," he said with a grin, then, touching her necklace, he asked, "Would you dislike it a great deal if I asked you not to wear that tonight?"

It was a heavy gold chain set with small emeralds and Ariel thought it matched her gown quite well; it was also a match for his ring. Still, she said, "No, certainly not. What would you prefer that I wear? Several of my necklaces would not do with this gown, but I have a plain gold one and another with three small diamonds."

"No necklace at all."

Ariel had unfastened the clasp as she spoke and now stared at him in surprise. The décolletage of her gown was rather deep and her shoulders bare, which made her feel rather undressed now that she had nothing at all about her neck, even though the necklace had hidden only a small part of her flesh.

She did not ask his reason, but Dexter said, "Just a conceit of mine, if you do not mind," and picked up her sable-trimmed evening cloak to lay it about her shoulders.

Still puzzled, she said again, "Certainly not, since you wish it," and as they passed Hodges, holding the door for them, she placed the necklace in his hands, saying, "Give this to Parsons, if you please, Hodges."

Hodges murmured agreement and looked after them, wondering to what sort of place the earl was planning to take her ladyship, that she did not dare to wear her jewels. His behavior was quite shameless, and her ladyship must be mad to permit it.

Lady Jersey bade them welcome and was well launched into one of her interminable monologues when Dexter, apparently becoming aware for the first time of the contrast between his hostess' bejeweled form and Ariel's bare throat, broke in contritely, "Oh Lord, I forgot. Come."

He drew Ariel into an alcove, as if attempting to be out of sight of the guests, although at least half a dozen of them could see the pair plainly and even Lady Jersey had to take no more than a step or two, which she did promptly, to be a witness at what was happening. She was quite out of patience with Dexter for having interrupted her and with Ariel for having been the cause of it.

"I had not forgotten, of course," Dexter was telling Ariel with a grin. "I planned it this way; I thought it the best way to attract the notice of everyone."

From his pocket he took a necklace whose magnificence drew a gasp from Ariel.

"My mother's diamonds. I am certain that at least half the crowd here this evening will recognize them. I hope that you will not mind that they are only a loan?"

"N-no. Certainly not. Oh, they are beautiful. I would not wish anything to happen to them."

"I shall see that it does not."

Stepping behind her, he drew the necklace about her throat and made certain the clasp was securely fastened. His hands then slipped to her shoulders and Ariel could feel his head bent toward hers. To the watchers, it would seem that he was kissing her neck.

She imagined that she could feel the touch of his lips and, hardly aware of what she was doing, she turned about and put up a hand to stroke his cheek.

"That was perfect," he murmured, catching her hand and pressing a kiss upon the palm. "Everyone who saw that caress will be certain that you meant it."

But I *did* mean it, she thought, as he drew her onto the floor to join the country dance which was just beginning. They separated in the movement of the dance, Ariel's mind whirling with confused thoughts.

Dexter – no, Randall – had believed that it was mere acting upon her part, as had she at the time; but she knew now that it had been more than that. She had wanted to caress him, had thrilled to the touch of his hands upon her shoulders, had ached to feel his lips, not upon her palm or neck – not that he had actually touched her neck, she had imagined that – but upon her willing mouth. Oh, she would know how to respond to his kiss if she received another.

She was, she told herself severely, behaving like a girl who was in love. But she *could not,* knowing that all of this was merely a charade, be in love with this handsome red-haired rake.

Or could she?

"No!" she said so suddenly that the gentleman opposite her at the moment looked at her in astonishment and she said quickly, "It is nothing. I but missed a step."

He nodded, smiling, and moved away, leaving Ariel to force herself to smile as she admitted for the first time that she was utterly, hopelessly in love with the Earl of Dexter.

She might have felt less hopeless had she been able to look into Dexter's house later that evening to see the earl wrestling with a dilemma of his own.

After taking Ariel home and persuading her, against all her arguments that it was too valuable to be risked, that she should keep the necklace for the time being, he had paid a surreptitious visit to an obliging Cyprian of his acquaintance, then had gone home, thinking wryly that to have a mistress in name only could be slightly inconvenient at times.

None of his friends, he was certain, would have believed that he and Ariel were not lovers. And if they could be brought to believe it, how they would roast him! Dexter, with his reputation, to be put off by a green girl.

Lady Ariel was a pleasant, as well as a beautiful companion. It amused him, too, to make her blush with his outrageous remarks. The young females of his acquaintance had long since forgotten how to blush, if indeed they had ever known. He was aware that Ariel was attracted to him and, with his considerable experience with ladies, he did not doubt his ability to make her his mistress in fact with only the slightest effort.

But was that what he wished? For all her efforts to appear a woman of the world, Ariel was only a girl, a veritable widgeon, who had tumbled into this coil through no fault of her own (but what about that bedroom?) and who had been harmed rather than helped by his interference in her life. He ought never to have suggested this disgraceful scheme to her, much less have permitted her to take part in it.

He remembered the night he had gone to her home with the intention of beginning the *affaire* which everyone suspected was well under way. She had been shocked by his behavior, indignant; but how soft her lips had felt when he had captured them, how they had trembled beneath his kiss. What a pleasure it would be to coax them to respond to his caress, to teach that little greenhead to love him.

Pausing in his pacing about the room, he kicked at an unoffending log in the grate, uncaring that he had marred his shoe. No, he did not want to make Ariel his mistress; but if he did not, what the devil *did* he want?

THIRTEEN

Peter Soames was an angry man. His wrath was divided between the Earl of Dexter for having submitted him to such a humiliating experience and Lady Ariel for having been the cause of the encounter. Many of his former friends were now shunning him, showing their disgust because he had failed to challenge Dexter after the man had knocked him down and then had merely walked away when the earl had publicly threatened to horsewhip him. In their minds, only a duel would erase the insult.

It would have pleased him to be able to challenge Dexter, but the earl's marksmanship was too well known; not that he was noted for duelling, but a man who could hit the wafer ten times out of ten could scarcely miss a target of his size. Soames did not *think* the earl would try to kill him if they met, but he could not be certain. Considering the man's hot temper, he might do so, depending upon his friendship with the Regent to save him from the consequences of his act. And even if the wound did not prove fatal, it would undoubtedly be painful and perhaps crippling.

He had not had a gun in his hands more than a score of times in his life and the less said about his marksmanship the better. The only way he would have a chance of coming out the victor in a meeting with Dexter would be to fire before the court and, even then, he could not be certain of success. At any rate, such an act would earn him more scorn than his present behavior. Even his brother's rank would not save him from being cut by the *ton;* it might become necessary for him to go abroad.

The more he thought about the matter, the more certain he became that the entire fault for his present predicament could be laid at the feet of Lady Ariel Laurence.

What right had she to go running to Dexter to complain of his actions merely because he had tried to kiss her (the fact that his intention had been to go far beyond kissing was conveniently forgotten)? If she had meant to play fast and loose with Dexter, she would not have encouraged other men

243

by going about in such revealing gowns. Had she not flaunted herself upon the ballroom floor and even strolled in the gardens with the Regent in an effort to trap him?

"If she had been able to entice the old man into offering her his protection," he muttered, "she would have given Dexter the go-by so quickly he would not have known what had happened."

He did not doubt that it was her disappointment in not attracting the Regent which had made her treat him in such a fashion. The blow she had struck had caused his nose to puff up so that he had felt it necessary to keep to his house for several days to avoid embarrassing questions, and he had only come out for the first time when Dexter had smashed him in the mouth, making two or three more days of retirement advisable.

"The jade is going to pay for that," he said angrily and set himself to planning how it might be best to avenge himself upon her.

His first thought had been to abduct her, for it would give him the greatest pleasure to have her at his mercy for several days. He decided against that idea quickly, however; if Dexter had threatened to horsewhip him merely for mentioning the lady's name, to what lengths might he go to settle accounts after such an act? The pleasure he might take in avenging himself upon her would hardly be worth the price he must pay for it. It would be best to keep his hands off Lady Ariel.

There was someone, he thought, someone else – someone whose well-being certainly would mean nothing to the earl, but whose ruin could be counted upon to bring her ladyship a great deal of pain. That milk and water miss who sometimes accompanied her. Despite the fact that she lived with Lady Ariel, he was almost certain that the girl was innocent and *could* be ruined by an abduction.

Also, he could visualize an extra pleasure in taking the younger girl. It had been some time since an innocent girl had come into his hands, all but the most callous of the madams having long since refused to allow him access to their new girls because of his extreme cruelty to them. Yes, what he would do to the little blonde would cause her cousin enough unhappiness to repay him for what he had suffered.

The two young ladies were seen together much less often now that Dexter had come to town, understandably, for what man would wish a third party about to witness his lovemaking? It occurred to Mr. Soames that he might have to wait a day or two to find the younger girl alone, but he was certain that it would happen and he could afford to wait.

Each afternoon at four of the clock, Lord Dexter's smart phaeton could be seen outside the house in Cavendish Square as his lordship called to take Ariel for a drive through the Park where they might be seen by the gossip-mongers of the *ton*. Almost every day, Ariel told herself that she would not go with him another time. It was agony, loving him as she did, to sit beside him, to have his hand holding hers as he helped her to the vehicle's seat and down again, to listen to the phrases which would convince passersby that they were besotted with one another – and to know that it meant nothing to him.

Still, she knew the agony would be worse if she did not see him, so she was always ready promptly when he called, aware of how he disliked to keep his cattle standing. The groom who would be at their heads as she came out of the house was always dismissed to kick his heels until they returned. It was his custom to stroll around to the stables for a visit with Fraser, to enjoy a glass of heavy wet and to compare notes about "their" comparative steeds.

Several days of loitering in the neighborhood, hoping that his presence would not be noticed, had shown Mr. Soames that he could count upon an hour or more before the pair returned and he made his plans accordingly. About ten minutes after they had left one afternoon, he directed his own carriage to the door and ordered his coachman to wait.

Hodges eyed this new caller with the same disapproval which he showed to all gentlemen who came to the house, with the exception of Mr. MacPherson, whom he trusted. However, he agreed to summon Miss Morwin when the newcomer said it was a matter of great urgency.

Clarissa came down the stairs, surprised to find that the caller was a stranger. She had a vague memory of having seen him at some time, but doubted that they had been introduced. When she paused, irresolute, Mr. Soames came toward her, hand outstretched.

"Miss Morwin, I beg of you to make haste. There has been an accident. Your cousin —"

"Ariel? Has she been hurt?"

"Quite badly, I fear. She has been asking for you. Let me take you to her."

Not doubting his words, for she had always mistrusted the safety of Lord Dexter's phaeton, Clarissa did not wait to fetch her bonnet or to answer Hodges' anxious questions, but ran down the steps. Mr. Soames was at her side and had the coach door opened for her at once. She was about to step within when she heard her name called by the voice she would always recognize.

Peter Soames had also heard the gentleman call out and placed his hand against Clarissa's back, trying to force her into the coach, but she caught at the edge of the door as she turned to face James MacPherson, who came hurrying up to her.

"Oh James," she called, "you have come just in time. Please come with me. I must go at once to Ariel, who has been hurt in an accident."

"Not unless it has occurred within the past three minutes," he said. "I passed Lord Dexter's phaeton, with Lady Ariel at his side, just before I turned into your street."

"I do not understand. This gentleman –"

"Who is no gentleman. I know who he is and he can mean you no good. You will not go with him, Clarissa."

James caught her arm as he spoke, but Mr. Soames gripped the other one and said angrily, "Stay out of this, whoever you might be. I say that the chit is going with me."

For the second time in less than a week, Mr. Soames found himself flat upon his back because of a blow to his mouth. Scrambling to his feet, he advanced upon the other, while Clarissa shrieked and cowered against the side of the carriage.

He was facing no one of Dexter's caliber

this time and Mr. Soames felt confident of his ability to conquer this young sprig, whom he must have outweighted by at least four stone. However, his excesses had left him in poor condition and James had the added incentive of fighting for his love. One blow merely grazed his cheek as he knocked the older man down a second time, then a third.

After this last blow, Mr. Soames showed no desire to return to the encounter, but ran around the far side of the carriage, clambered up beside the driver and swore at him to get his cattle moving. Clarissa turned to her rescuer, her eyes shining.

"Oh, you were wonderful," she said breathlessly, then, "Oh, you are hurt. Come, let me tend to you."

James walked silently beside her into the house, where she sent the servants to scurrying about to bring water and medications, snapping orders in a manner quite unlike herself. This, however, was for James, and for him she could be as bold as anyone. Tenderly, she cleansed his cheek and his bruised knuckles.

"I think they should be bandaged," she said anxiously, but he replied with some impatience,

"No – it is nothing serious. Leave them be. Now, I wish to talk with you, Clarissa –

249

alone." His tone and the look which accompanied it caused Hodges to herd the others ahead of him out of the room, thinking that he had never known the usually calm young Mr. MacPherson to be in such a taking.

"I wish to talk to you," James repeated as the door closed behind the servants.

"Certainly James. What is it? Oh, I was so proud of you."

He made an impatient gesture. "You ought not to have been forced to see such a thing. I fear I was not thinking. I ought to have sent you into the house before I struck him."

"I am happy that you did not; it was wonderful to watch how easily you defeated him, and he so much larger than you. I do not know what I should have done if you had not come when you did."

"Clarissa, will you listen to me?"

"Certainly, my dear, I am listening. But what could he have meant by telling me such a tale?"

"He meant you no good, dear one; it is best that you do not know more than that about him. But that is what I wish to speak to you about."

"About him? But I do not even know him, James. Surely you cannot believe that I would encourage –"

"Of course I do not. I feel I know you

250

too well to think that you would ever offer encouragement to one of his sort. But he is a libertine of the worst kind and a part of the crowd with which your cousin has embroiled herself. I dislike speaking so about any lady, but Lady Ariel is becoming notorious. Only look at the manner in which she has been conducting herself with Lord Dexter."

Although astonished that James, who was customarily the soul of politeness, could be offering any criticism of her dear Ariel, Clarissa could not help laughing at that charge.

"That means nothing at all," she told him. "Ariel explained it to me. 'Tis all a pretence to deceive –"

"To deceive *you*, if she told you such a story as that." He spoke in a stern tone which she would not have believed possible for her mild-mannered James. "One has only to look at the pair of them to know the truth of their relationship. That is why you must come away with me, Clarissa – and at once. Let me take you to my aunt, who will care for you until we can be married."

"Away? Oh no. I cannot leave Ariel."

"You must do so in time, my dear. And it is best that you come now, before she has a chance to draw you down to her level."

His concern for her was so deep that he had

completely forgotten that her cousin was one of the firm's wealthiest clients; but even had he remembered, the result would have been the same. Clarissa must be saved from her and her companions.

"How dare you speak so of her to me – or to anyone? Ariel is everything that is good and kind."

"She may once have been so, but she has changed since she came to London. You must have noticed that. That man today who tried to carry you off – he is part of the crowd she runs with, rakes and worse. She cannot any longer be thought a fit companion for you."

Clarissa stamped her foot. "Ariel is all the companion I require – now or ever," she said angrily. "And if she is not good enough for you to know, neither am I."

She tore off the ring with its tiny stone, which until this moment had been her most cherished possession, flung it at him, and, ignoring his calls, raced up the stairs to her bedroom, where she threw herself upon the bed, sobbing. James took several steps after her, then stopped. Clarissa had made her choice. He searched the floor for the ring, pocketed it, and walked slowly out of the house.

Drawing his pair to a standstill before the house in Cavendish Square half an hour later, as his groom, who had judged the time of his master's return to the minute, came forward to take the horses' heads till her ladyship alit, Dexter said, "We have a most amusing invitation for this evening, my dear. Having finally despaired of me it seems, Lady Soames has snaffled poor Frank Mapes for her daughter. I have heard that tonight's ball is by way of being a betrothal party."

So he was free of that danger; there was no need for the charade to be continued any longer. Dully, Ariel said, "You must know that Lady Soames would never invite me to her ball. She disapproved of me even before –"

"Even before she knew the 'truth' about us?" Dexter asked with a cheerfulness which made her struggle to keep back the tears. "Well, you may be certain that she has seen to it that *I* received an invitation – just so that I might see what I have missed by not offering for Myrtle. As if I did not know that very well enough already, and thank my stars and you for that. I made it quite plain to her that I should not attend if I could not have your company, so I bear an invitation from her ladyship for you as well."

The temptation to say that she would go was very strong. It would mean one more evening in his company, one more time to feel

253

his arm about her during the waltz, to receive the attentions which she alone knew were false — but knowing it would be the last time they would share these moments, Ariel feared that she could not go through the evening without breaking down. The only thing which would save her pride now was that he would never know how much she had come to love him. It would be unbearable if he knew that she was another of his conquests.

"Yes, I can see that you would have to tell her that," she agreed, "but I am sorry; I do not wish to enter Lady Soames' home under any circumstances, even to help you show how little you care for having missed the chance to wed her daughter."

"You need not fear to encounter Peter Soames; I am certain that he will not be there for her ladyship would not welcome him. Even his own family has no good opinion of him."

"It is not that," she protested, wondering if she would be able to hold back her tears until she reached the safety of the house. "I simply do not care for her ladyship any more than she cares for me. Also, I fear I have been neglecting my cousin too much of late. I think it would be the best thing for me to stay at home with her this evening."

"As you wish." By his tone, one would

have thought that he was disappointed by her refusal, but Ariel was aware of how well he could pretend his part. He held her hand as if unwilling to let her go and kissed her fingers, although there was no one to see except his groom. She remembered how he had said, "Servants will gossip." Well, soon there would be nothing more for them to gossip about.

"But you will ride with me tomorrow as usual?" he asked as she withdrew her hand and turned toward the steps.

So he intended to carry on the play for a time. Of course. If he ended it too abruptly now, people might suspect that it had been a pose. Ariel nodded, forcing a smile. Not trusting herself to speak, she hurried into the house.

Dexter was disappointed that she had not wished to accompany him this evening. He had been aware of the change in Ariel's attitude from the moment he had told her of Myrtle Soames' engagement. He had begun to think that she had been enjoying his company as much as he had enjoyed hers. Now it would seem that she was only too happy for an opportunity to bring the charade to an end.

He swore at himself for not having made an effort before this to convince her that his interest in her was no longer an assumed one. It would be far more difficult to do so now that she could see no further need for going out with him. There was no question but that he had made a mull of the entire business. He slapped the lines down across the backs of the startled horses, and when his groom dared to mutter a protest, gave that luckless individual so violent a tongue-lashing that he expected to find himself turned off before the day was out.

Within the house, Ariel slipped quickly past Hodges, not replying to his greeting, and hurried up the stairs. As she neared her room, she could hear the sound of weeping from the bedroom across the hall. Opening the door quietly, she saw Clarissa crumpled upon the bed, sobbing wildly. Her own grief put aside for the moment at the sight of her cousin's woe, Ariel sat beside her and gathered Clarissa into her arms.

"What is it, dear? What is troubling you?"

"I want to die," Clarissa wailed, soaking the shoulder of Ariel's gown with her tears.

"But what has made you feel this way?" Clare had always had a great deal of sensibility, but it was unlike her to be in such a taking as this and Ariel was quite concerned.

"I – it is James."

"James? But, dear, I thought that you were so happy with him."

"I th-thought so, too," Clarissa said with a hiccup, "b-but I was quite deceived in him."

What could James MacPherson – who had always appeared to be a pattern-card of respectability – have done to overset the girl in this manner? Ariel could not think that he would have frightened her cousin by violent lovemaking or improper suggestions.

"I did not know he c-could be so unfeeling and unk-kind. You would not believe h-how he behaved today."

"Now, dry your eyes, dear," Ariel soothed, "and tell me all about it. Certainly, it cannot be as bad as all that."

Drying her eyes seemd to be a waste of time, for the tears continued to come, but less heavily than before and, after blowing her nose, Clarissa was able to pull herself together enough that she could tell of the horrible man who had come to the house with the story that Ariel had been injured and of how he had tried to force Clarissa into his coach after she had discovered he was lying.

From her description, Ariel had little trouble in recognizing the would-be abductor as Peter Soames and exclaimed in anger at his behavior toward her cousin, although she did not understand that he had planned this in an attempt to revenge himself upon her. When she heard of how Mr. MacPherson had routed the older man, she said heartily:

"How very brave of him – when the other man was so much larger than he. But it is only the sort of thing I should have expected of him. Surely you can find no fault with that."

"No. Oh no. He thought that I ought not to have seen it, but I was happy that I did so, for he behaved so wonderfully – then. It was af-af-terwards." She began to sob again, harder than before.

"But what could he have done?" Certainly the young man could not have thought that Clare would have encouraged such a man, that she had been going with him willingly, even if it might have looked that way at first. Anyone who knew the girl even slightly could not be so mistaken in her character.

"It was what he s-said – that I should come away from here and stay with his aunt t-till we were married. That, with friends like that m-man and Lord Dexter, you were not a fit companion for me."

Ariel was aghast. When she had agreed to his lordship's scheme, it had been with her usual impulsiveness, giving no thought to the outcome. She had known that she would be laying herself open to censure by appearing to encourage Lord Dexter's attentions as she

258

had been doing, but she was already being censured through no fault of her own. Even farther from her mind than the thought that she might fall in love with the earl was the idea that any of her actions might reflect unfavorably upon her cousin.

She felt that she must even hold herself responsible for today's action by Peter Soames. Her reaction to his advances had, she believed, discouraged him from thinking of her as a light woman until Lord Dexter had come into her life with his mad scheme. Doubtless he thought the worst of her after that – but how could *anyone* think such a thing of sweet little Clare?

"Do you mean that your quarrel with James was because of *me?*"

"Y-yes. I told him that if you were not good enough for him to know, then neither was I. And I gave him back his ring. Ohhh." She buried her head on Ariel's sodden shoulder.

Ariel sighed. Despite his kindness in offering to take her up for a drive on the morrow, she knew that Lord Dexter had no further need for her now that Myrtle Soames could no longer be wished upon him. And since her presence in London would continue to be barrier between her cousin and the man she loved, there was only one thing to be done.

"Listen to me, Clare," she said briskly. "You are going to get up at once and bathe your eyes. You are quite ruining them with all this crying. Then you are going to write a note to James, telling him that you are sorry for the way you acted this afternoon and ask him to forgive you. I am certain that he will be only too willing to do so."

"Never!" Clarissa said furiously. "Why should I ask forgiveness when it was he who was at fault, not I? When he said all those horrible things about you –"

"They were unkind, I admit – but do you not see, dear, that he was doubtless overset by the danger you had been in and by the fight he had just had with Mr. So – with the gentleman who tried to carry you off? I am certain he did not mean the things he was saying. In fact, he may not even have realized that he had said them, but, being a gentleman, he will not wish to say that he was wrong. So you must do so, even if you know that you were not, so that everything will be well between you again. You love him as much as ever, do you not?"

"No – oh yes, yes. I do. But I cannot tell him so, for he will wish to take me away – and I *will* not leave you, Ariel."

"But of course you must do so when you and James are married, so if you do so now, does it really matter so much? In fact, if he wishes for you to stay with his aunt for a time, that will solve my problem. I have been wondering what I ought to do."

Her mind was working furiously, trying to find a way to convince Clare that to go to James' aunt would be the best thing for both of them. "I knew that you would not wish to leave James, and I have decided that I am going home."

"Going home? But I thought – I thought you *liked* it here."

"Oh, I have enjoyed myself immensely." She fetched a moistened cloth and began to bathe her cousin's swollen eyes as she spoke. "But I fear I have been trotting too hard these past weeks. The quiet of the country is exactly what I need for a time."

"Then I shall go with you," Clarissa said loyally.

"How could you bear not to see James again?" And how can *you* bear, her heart asked, not to see Randall again? I can bear it better, her mind answered, never to see him again than to be forced to see him with someone else.

Clarissa hesitated. If Ariel was determined to leave London, she felt that she should go with her. Still, that would mean never seeing James again – and, although that was what she

261

had told him she wished, she knew it was not so.

"You see," Ariel was saying, "I have been wondering what I should do about you if I left, for you could not stay here alone. But if James' aunt is willing to look after you, it will ease my mind."

She disliked sounding so selfish, but it was necessary to convince her cousin that she would not be needed, would, in fact, be in the way.

Clarissa looked hurt at first, then, to Ariel's surprise broke into a laugh.

"I know what it is. I was fooled for a time, thinking you might be interested in Lord Dexter – but you did tell me that you were going about with him only as a pretense. You are going home to marry Henry."

"I told him we would speak of it when I came home," Ariel said, happy that Clare had hit upon a solution which pleased her.

But to marry Henry – when she loved Randall?

FOURTEEN

Even in the depths of her unhappiness, Ariel could not fail to appreciate the difference in the comfort of her return journey over the one she had made to London. Instead of the rickety rig and the single horse, she was settled in her modish carriage – so well-sprung that it made light of the ruts – with Fraser and a groom in attendance, and with no hesitation upon the part of a landlord to provide the best in his house for one who was able to travel in such luxury, although privately he might question the wisdom of a lady traveling with no female servant.

Parsons had admitted that she had little liking for the country; still, she would have accompanied her mistress. However, there would be neither room nor need for her in Sylvester's small house. Giving the woman her wage for two months, Ariel bade her enjoy herself till her return.

Later, she would write to James MacPherson, ordering him to pay off the servants, giving those who wished to apply for positions elsewhere a good character, and to dispose of her carriage and horses. Knowing how deeply James had come to disapprove of her, she wondered if it would not be better for her to write to his father instead. Still, that would imply that she had been dissatisfied with the manner in which James had handled her affairs, which was not so. She would not wish to cause any trouble for the man Clare was to marry; and, in any case, James would doubtless be so happy to have her far away from Clare that he would do whatever she asked.

The thought of marriage brought Henry to mind. No word had come from him during the time she was in London and she could not know if he was of the same mind. Even if she still wished it, could she become his wife, loving Randall as she did? Could she submit to his caresses when every fiber of her being called out for those of a red-haired rake? Would it be fair to Henry for her to do so?

She had argued the question in her mind at least a hundred times and had reached no conclusion by the time she alighted from the carriage before the modest house and overpaid the servants generously before sending them back to London.

"Would it not be best if we stayed, my lady?" Fraser asked anxiously. "You will need us when you return to the city."

"There is no room for you here and I shall

not return soon," she told him. "There will be time enough to send word."

It was cowardly, but she could not bring herself to tell those who had served her so well that she did not intend to return at all. James would have to dismiss them for her; she must remember to tell him to deal with them generously. She could ask Clare to have her gowns and fripperies packed and sent to her, although she did not know what use she would have for her London finery here.

Perhaps instead of marrying Henry, she would travel. That would mean that she would have to find a companion. At the moment, the idea had no more appeal for her than any of the others which had come to mind. The only one which could appeal was so impossible that she must not think of it.

She could scarcely tell Henry baldly that she had come home to marry him, but would go to call upon him, asking him if he would like to purchase the estate, since he had always wanted it. If he agreed to buy, she would sell it and go away, but if he asked her again to marry him, she would accept and would try to make him a good wife. There would be no need for him to know that she did not love him, although she doubted if it would matter greatly to him that she did not, as long as she came so well dowered.

She was somewhat shocked when she first saw him. In so short a time, how could she have forgotten so completely what he looked like? When they were growing up together, she had thought him almost handsome. Doubtless he was, but with the image of Dexter beside him, amber eyes mocking her, Henry seemed insignificant.

"So you've come back," he said without a greeting.

"Yes." Should she ask him at once if he wished to buy the land or would it be best if they talked for a time first? He gave her no time to decide which course to take.

"You have left it a bit late, have you not?" he asked. "I wished to marry you when your uncle died; you knew that I had wished it since we were children. But no – you must go off to London and flaunt yourself there among the fops and dandies. Do you think that word of the way you have been misbehaving has not even reached back here to us? Now, when your fancy lord has tired of you, you come back and think I would still marry you. Let me tell you, my lady, *my* wife must be a decent woman."

"Oh –" Ariel could say no more, could not even suggest selling him the estate. She truly had not wished to marry Henry. She would never wish to marry anyone except the Earl of Dexter, and he did not want her. Now it seemed that Henry did not want her either.

She turned to go and it occurred suddenly to Henry just what he had tossed aside so ruthlessly.

"Wait," he called. Ariel stopped and allowed him to come up with her, wondering if he had thought of something else to add to his denunciation of her character.

"I have heard talk of how you tossed your money about while you were in London, money which could have been put to better use here. I suppose that most of it is gone now. But do you still have the land – your uncle's land?"

"Yes," she said dully. "I still have it."

She had thought he would want it; she would make him give her a good price for it and would send all the money to Clare, telling her that it was her share of the estate. It would make a nice dowry, but would not be so much that James could object to it.

"Very well, then – I'll marry you."

Ariel whirled to face him, eyes blazing.

"So now you will marry me, will you? As long as I have the estate, I am decent enough to become your wife. Let me tell you something, Henry Drayling – I had intended to offer to sell you the land. But now you will never get your hands upon as much as an inch

267

of it. And I would not marry you even if I *did* have to be married."

She turned and fled along the lane, tears of anger blinding her until she could scarcely see her way, eager only to reach the sanctuary of the old house. The London beaux – even Peter Soames – had wanted her for herself, no matter how dishonorable their purpose had been. She found Henry's offer more insulting than any of theirs.

As she approached the house, a tall figure arose from the step and came to meet her.

"What do you mean, running off from me in that manner?" Lord Dexter demanded.

This was outside of enough! How dare he come here to taunt her when she was already so miserable?

"Oh, go away," she told him crossly. "There is no one down here to be impressed with our play-acting. I did what you wished. And my reputation is ruined, even here, so there is nothing more you can do to me. You ought to be satisfied."

He caught her shoulders, giving her a sharp shake.

"Your reputation was in shreds, my sweet," he told her sternly, "before I arrived upon the scene. You managed to do that quite well, with no help from me. But who will give a snap of their fingers about any gossip of the past when you are the Countess of Dexter?"

"What?"

"I am doing what I once said I would not do, making you an offer in form, my dear. I trust you will not wish me to go down upon my knees. I shall do so if that is what it will take to make you happy, but I fear that the path is rather dusty."

Ariel choked upon a laugh that was half a sob.

"Only you, Randall Vernon, could worry about getting dirt upon your – your clothing while in the middle of a proposal. It was kind of you to come and make an offer, but there is no need."

"There is every need, especially when I learned from your cousin that you have come back here with the intention of marrying some farmer. I could not permit you to do that. There has not been a moment since we began our charade that I have not wanted to catch you up and carry you away. Not as my mistress, but as my wife. Do you have the least idea, you vexatious creature, of how very much I love you?"

He might have convinced himself that those had always been his intentions, but Ariel was not deceived. With perfect honesty, she said, "No, I have no way of knowing –"

She was not permitted to finish for he

had caught her up into an embrace which threatened to crush her ribs and his lips were upon hers.

Ariel had thought that she remembered how wonderful his kiss could be, but she knew now that memory was a pale thing compared to reality. The earth beneath her feet, the trees, the buildings – everything had faded away; nothing was left in the world except the two of them and the ecstasy of knowing that Randall loved her.

Dexter was similarly wrapped up in this enchantment and neither of them was aware of the figure approaching up the lane until Henry said harshly, "You do not waste time, do you? If I do not greet you as you think I ought, you can find another quickly enough."

Still held tightly in her lover's embrace, Ariel turned her head to look at him dreamily, her bruised lips giving evidence of having been thoroughly and delightfully kissed.

"Oh – Henry," she said as if surprised to find that such a person as he still existed in her world. "This is the Earl of Dexter." That was not the way she ought to have made the presentation, she knew, but she was not given the chance to correct it.

"Who does not appreciate the manner in which you have just addressed his future wife," Dexter was saying. "You may be interested to know that I recently threatened to horsewhip a man who said something of the same about her. I do not know you, but I am willing to see that you receive the same treatment."

The menace in his tone and the glare which accompanied the words caused Henry to take a step backward and say hastily, "Oh, I fear I misunderstood. I must wish you both happy."

"Oh, we shall be," Ariel assured him, remaining – quite brazenly, Henry thought – in Dexter's arms.

"One reason that I am so happy," she told him rashly, "is that I did not offer you the chance to purchase this land, as I had intended to do. It seems that the earl has the most wonderful idea. He is planning to turn the estate into a hunting club."

Henry looked at the pair of them in horror and Dexter, putting Ariel aside for a moment, said smoothly, "Oh, do not talk like such a widgeon, my love. The – er – gentleman must know that this is not hunting country."

Ariel shot him an angry look for spoiling her revenge upon Henry, but as if he was unaware of having said anything which displeased her, Dexter went on, "You must forgive the girl, sir, for you know how it is. I have never yet seen a lady who was capable of understanding these matters. What I am planning for this

271

property is not a hunting club, but rather a sporting club for gentlemen who wish to enjoy such things away from the din of the city, but who do not wish to invite their friends to their own estates.

"I think that would be the perfect spot to build the race course." He pointed to the field which Henry had always visualized as being planted to turnips. "And I had thought of setting up an outdoor shooting gallery as well; it is a novel idea, but I think it would prove to be quite popular. I should warn you, however, that it might be wise to keep your animals away from this area when practice begins, for I fear that some of the younger gentlemen are apt to shoot wide of the mark – especially if they happen to be foxed."

"Oh yes, you must be careful, Henry," Ariel put in. "It would be terrible if some of them were to shoot your lambs."

"We certainly would not wish that to happen. It would be best if you were to pen them as far away from the boundary as possible. You will have to put in more fences, anyhow, when we tear out the hedgerows to widen the lane. It would make an excellent race course for curricles."

Unable to listen to any more talk of a plan which he considered to be the desecration of good farming land, Henry backed away, then turned and nearly ran back to his house, determined to gather his neighbors at once to protest the building of such a club in their part of the country.

Dexter once more slipped an arm about Ariel and, feeling his body shaking with laughter, she looked up at him to ask, "Are you really planning to do all that?"

"Certainly not. I can think of nothing which would be less suitable – unless it would be your idea of a hunting lodge. Do you think that even he would have believed that for a moment? But I could see that you wish to throw a fright into him for some reason, so I thought that I might oblige."

"I think he *might* have believed me about the hunting but your idea was so much the better one. Did you see how he was shaking like a blanc-mange? Do you know how wonderful you are, my lord?"

"No – but I shall expect you to tell me so at least a dozen times a day for the rest of our lives."

"Only if I am repaid for the compliment," Ariel said pertly.

"In what way?"

"Like this." She slipped her arms about his neck and raised her lips invitingly, but Dexter laid a finger across them, shaking his head.

"No, there are several matters which must

be settled first. Such as the matter of the strange bedroom in your house."

"Strange – bedroom?"

"Yes. The one which I was informed that you were keeping in readiness for me – or for some other gentleman, since I knew that it could not be mine."

Ariel wrinkled her brow, then burst into laughter.

"How did they – oh, one of my guests must have gone on a spying visit which does not surprise me at all – and found it. *That* was only Sir Percy's room."

"And who is Sir Percy? No kin of yours, I'll wager."

There was a note in his voice which boded no good for the unknown gentleman. Ariel thrilled to this sign of his jealousy, but laughed again as she explained.

"No – Sir Percy Rawls is the owner of the house. James MacPherson allowed us to hire it when Sir Percy was forced to flee to the country to escape his creditors. We never saw him, of course, but he had left some things in his room. Do you mean that –"

"– was apparently the item which started the worst of the gossip about you. Sally Jersey assured me that you had prepared it for my return to the city, but as I knew she was mistaken, you can imagine my feelings toward the unknown who had been so favored."

"*You* were jealous? Good!"

"How can you say that?"

"Because I am happy to know that you are. It is some payment for the agonies I have suffered thinking that you cared nothing for me. But now," she raised her lips once more, "what of my wage?"

"You must earn it – do you remember?"

"You are wonderful," she said softly, "Wonderfu –" and was repaid with an enthusiasm which carried both of them whirling away into a world where no such things as disputed lands or jealous neighbors could exist – a world where there was only the pair of them and their love.